FURY AT BENT FORK

What becomes known as the Stone Creek Valley war starts with one word: Guilty. Eager to get their hands on his father's ranch, the Committee — the four biggest ranchers in the area — send Chad Hunter to jail on a trumped-up charge of cattle rustling. Upon his release a year later, he's got his work cut out for him, with the Committee's hired thugs terrorizing the area. When his brother is lynched and his father shot down, Hunter loads his guns and prepares to deal out his own brand of justice . . .

B. S. DUNN

FURY AT BENT FORK

Complete and Unabridged

LINFORD
Leicester

First published in Great Britain in 2016 by
Robert Hale
an imprint of The Crowood Press
Wiltshire

First Linford Edition
published 2019
by arrangement with
The Crowood Press
Wiltshire

A catalogue record for this book is available
from the British Library.

ISBN 978–1–4448–4207–4

Published by
F. A. Thorpe (Publishing)
Anstey, Leicestershire

Set by Words & Graphics Ltd.
Anstey, Leicestershire
Printed and bound in Great Britain by
T. J. International Ltd., Padstow, Cornwall

This book is printed on acid-free paper

This one is for Sam and Jacob.

1

What became known as the Stone Creek Valley war started with one word: 'Guilty'.

This word was reluctantly uttered by the jury foreman in the trial of Chad Hunter, accused of rustling the Committee's cattle. The use of the word 'trial' in these circumstances would indicate the determination of a person's guilt or innocence by due process of the law. In this instance however, 'railroaded' would have been a more appropriate word.

It did not matter that the defence had a witness who could place Hunter ten miles from the scene of the alleged crime. The Committee had two who swore on the Bible that they had seen him with the cattle. It had not helped that the cattle were found hidden in a makeshift corral in Aspen Gulch, among the tall silver-barked trees on his father's land, and that most of the jury consisted of ranch hands who worked for the Committee. The result therefore was a foregone conclusion.

Chad Hunter was what some towns-folk branded a hellraiser. He was twenty-five and wiry. His shoulders were broad but without much meat on them. He was 6 feet 4 tall, with brown eyes and hair to match. His face was chiselled and his skin tanned from working in the sun. He was fast with a gun, had killed a man in a gunfight at the Red Jack saloon, wouldn't walk away from a fight and to be fair to the young man, no one would have called him a rustler. Whatever trouble he'd been in over the years, being an outlaw was not the cause. Some had whispered privately that it was only a matter of time, but they were few and far between.

Stone Creek Valley, Colorado was home to the town of Bent Fork, sited on the aptly named Stone Creek. The valley was a wide expanse of high country grazing land, lined and dotted throughout with stands of spruce, aspen, ponderosa, Douglas fir and lodgepole pine. Surrounded with high, snow-capped peaks and low, tree-lined ridges, the valley was also home to a vast variety of animal species such as elk, mule deer and white-tailed deer. Further up the ridges one could find black bears and the odd mountain lion or grey wolf. Stone Creek itself was the only water source in the lush valley and being so, all of the ranches touched the creek at some point to provide water for their cattle.

The Committee had themselves a plan for Stone Creek Valley and implementation started the day sheriff Joe Stern arrived at the Hunter ranch with a posse to arrest Chad. Now, as the courtroom erupted in uproar over the decision, only one man smiled outwardly: Hiram Yates, head of the Cattleman's Committee.

'No!' cried Pam Holder, her large

blue eyes instantly wet as tears filled them, then overflowed down her pale cheeks.

'Silence!' Judge Eldred Banks called out across the din while he banged his gavel. 'I must have order.'

Hunter looked across at Pam. She was his girl and at that very moment he wished he could take her slim frame in his arms and tell her that everything would be OK, but he wasn't so sure. He'd been found guilty of a crime that was punishable by ten years in prison. A crime that he didn't commit.

Next, Hunter's gaze settled on his own family. His mother wept silently while his father and brother seethed openly at the mockery of the court. Then he saw Hiram Yates. The fat man sat there with a large, toothy smile on his flabby face. He had on a grey suit of clothes. He always wore grey. Their eyes met across the room and Hunter felt positive that if he hadn't been manacled, he would've launched himself across the court and rammed those

4

damn teeth down the son of a bitch's throat.

Hunter looked back at Pam who dabbed at her eyes with a white handkerchief. She felt his gaze on her and looked up. Their eyes locked and then her gaze dropped, as tears flowed freely once more.

'I said order!' Judge Banks banged his little wooden hammer even harder.

Slowly the noise level dropped until it faded away and the packed courtroom became silent once more.

'That's better,' Banks nodded jerkily. 'Now, the jury is dismissed.'

Banks watched as the twelve men rose from the wooden bench seats and moved to the back of the room, where they waited for him to pass sentence.

'Right.' Banks' eyes settled on the accused. 'Stand up please, Mr Hunter.'

The chains of the manacles jingled as Hunter rose to his feet and stretched to his full height.

'Do you have anything to say before I pass sentence?'

Hunter shook his head. 'No sir, I guess everythin' that was meant to be said was said durin' the trial.'

Banks nodded. 'Let's get to it then, shall we?'

Hunter fixed his stare on the man who was about to pass sentence on him. His Honour Eldred Banks was sixty years old and had been the Bent Fork town judge for as long as Hunter could remember. He was of average height and build but his advanced years had changed his face into a wrinkled map of lines and creases. His hair was grey and he still carried his frame erect despite his age, but there was one thing that Hunter knew about the judge: the man was fair.

'Mr Hunter,' Banks started, 'you have been found guilty by your peers, of the crime of cattle rustling. This crime carries a sentence of ten years in the state penitentiary. By rights, that should be the punishment you receive, but, throughout the trial and especially on the evidence with which you were convicted, it seems to me that an air of doubt still hangs over these proceedings.'

Banks paused and a murmur rippled through the gathering.

'But alas you were found guilty and I am compelled to give you a custodial sentence, so, Chad Hunter you are therefore sentenced to one year at Hell's Creek penitentiary. Sentence is to commence immediately. Sheriff, take Mr Hunter away.'

With that, Judge Eldred Banks banged his gavel and ended proceedings.

★ ★ ★

Later that afternoon, Hunter was visited by his family and Pam. All were upset by the verdict handed down, but they also acknowledged that the outcome could have been far worse.

After they had left, Sheriff Joe Stern came into the cells from the front office. He was fifty years old, solid built and had been sheriff of Bent Fork for fifteen years. Age was catching up to him but he still had what it took to uphold the law in town.

'I'm sorry son,' he said, surprising Hunter.

'What for?'

'I never told anyone this before, but I believed you when you said you never stole them cattle.'

Hunter shook his head and waved his hand about as he indicated the small, damp cell. 'Fat lot of good you sayin' it now.'

Stern nodded. 'Hell son, I tried. I looked into everythin' I could to prove your story but when you buck a stacked deck, well . . . '

His voice trailed away. Hunter knew what Stern meant. The jury had been rigged from the start and no amount of evidence was going to change the outcome of the trial.

'Yeah,' Hunter allowed, 'I know.'

'So did the judge, son,' the sheriff explained. 'If he thought for one minute you were guilty, he'd would've given you them ten years.'

There was a silence between the two men before the sheriff spoke again. 'There is one thing that still puzzles me though. Why set you up like that? What do they get out of it?'

Hunter shrugged. 'I wish I knew, Joe.'

★   ★   ★

A week later, Chad Hunter sat in the back of a rickety tumbleweed wagon along with three other prisoners bound for the Hell's Creek penitentiary. Two marshals sat up front on a timber-backed bench seat while one other rode drag on a big chestnut horse. The wagon had been on the trail for five days.

'There she is, fellers,' a marshal on the front seat called back over his shoulder. 'Hell's Creek pen. Your new home.'

Their conveyance hit a rock and jerked over it. Inside, the other two prisoners lurched with the wagon and crashed against each other.

'Steady on, Willie,' one of the prisoners complained to the driver.

The marshals ignored him and kept their eyes to the front. Hunter looked out through the iron bars and across the green landscape to the large, block built prison that sat on a low hill. It overlooked the deep gorge through which Hell's Creek flowed. On the ridge line behind the prison, an ugly scar stood out clearly in contrast to the natural landscape. This was the quarry where convicts spent their days digging rock. The prison was to be his home for the next twelve months.

As their wagon rolled slowly across a large, timber trestle bridge that spanned the steep-sided gorge, Hunter looked down at the creek below. It was a roiling mass of white water, pierced by sharp granite peaks. The wagon lumbered up the trail on the other side, the horses strained at the harnesses as they climbed the hill. Once at the top, the trail levelled out and drew up to a large pair of rust-coloured, solid iron gates, pocked with large steel bolts that held them together.

One of the marshals called out to a man in a large, block guard tower. There was a brief exchange before a great rumble echoed from the surrounding ridges as the heavy gates slowly swung open. Then, as prey enters the jaws of a giant animal, the tumbleweed wagon rolled into the belly of the beast.

2

'Prisoner 85637, Warden wants to see you,' the burly guard announced to Chad Hunter as he swung the hammer down onto the rocky ground one more gruelling time. The iron head smashed into the dark grey rock, which split and sprayed a small shower of stone splinters over the rough ground. Hunter looked up from his work. 'What's he want?'

The guard shrugged heavy-set shoulders. 'How should I know? Just hurry up.'

Hunter dropped the sledge and straightened up. His wiry frame had filled out from the daily grind of work in the quarry and was now a rock-hard mass of muscle. Around the open cut pit men worked laboriously and the sound of hammer on stone echoed from the scarred rock face. It had been eight months since he'd first arrived at Hell's Creek pen. Eight long, hard months, throughout which Hunter had served mostly as a model prisoner. There had been some issues along the way and he now had the scars to prove it, but with only four months left of his incarceration, he meant to keep his nose clean.

'What does he want, Theodore?' Hunter asked the guard again as he followed him out of the stone quarry.

'I told you I don't know, but it could be somethin' to do with what happened to Luther.'

Luther was a guard who had been attacked by an animal named Killer Creel. Given name Bobby, but no one called him that, if they wanted to live. That was the almost fatal mistake Luther had made and Creel had attacked him for it. If it hadn't been for Hunter, the guard would be dead instead of in the infirmary. Ironically, that's exactly where Creel ended up after Hunter had smashed him senseless with a fist-sized rock. Word was that the big, shaggy-headed outlaw with the livid scar on his face swore black and blue when he woke up that he was going to kill the son of a bitch who'd put him there. Luther though would survive.

★ ★ ★

'Come on in, Hunter.' Warden Gates waved him over as he entered the office.

He looked about and knew it hadn't changed since his last visit. The timber furnishings, the pictures on the walls, it was all the same.

'Take a seat,' Gates offered and pointed to a wooden chair on the opposite side of the hardwood desk he sat at. 'That'll be all, Theodore.'

'Do you want him chained first, Boss?' the guard asked warily.

Gates shook his head. 'That won't be necessary, chains are for prisoners — Hunter here is being released.'

'Yes sir,' said Theodore and closed

the door behind him.

Hunter wasn't sure whether he'd heard Gates right. 'Did you say released, sir?'

'Yes, Hunter, I did say that,' Gates confirmed.

He was confused. 'But why? I still have four months to go.'

'You are being released because I see fit to make it happen,' Gates explained. 'You have been a relatively model prisoner, you've worked hard, kept out of trouble and the other day you saved the life of one of my guards. Besides, if you stay for another four months, Creel will try to kill you. So look at it as me returning the favour that you did for Luther.'

So many emotions ran through Hunter, he just stared at Gates. Dare he believe it? He looked into the warden's eyes and searched for any hint of a cruel joke.

'Don't you have anything to say?' Gates asked.

'I don't know what to say,' Hunter said, still numb with disbelief.

'I'll have to notify Sheriff Stern of your release,' Gates allowed. 'I presume you'll go back home?'

Hunter nodded. 'Yes sir.'

'Fine, I'll notify him and write you a letter that will basically say that you've served your time and are now a free man.'

'Thank you, Warden.'

'Just don't come back, Hunter.'

Two hours later, the rust-coloured iron gates that had admitted him to Hell's Creek penitentiary opened once more; Chad Hunter walked through a free man. He had been supplied with clean clothes and enough money to get him home to Bent Fork. Hunter smiled, overjoyed with his liberation. What he didn't realise then was that he had just walked out of one hell to ride into another.

★ ★ ★

The town of Bent Fork was bathed in the bright sunlight of a high country

16

spring. The snow had melted from the surrounding hills and the white landscape had been replaced with a lush green of new grass and spotted throughout with colourful wild flowers. Bent Fork itself was a thriving cattle town. Every business in it turned a good profit, which was the reason that the Cattleman's Committee had started to buy up the more lucrative ones. Pretty soon, the Committee would hold a monopoly on the best businesses in town, and Hiram Yates would become the most influential man in Bent Fork.

Four Committee men sat around a scarred table in the poorly lit back room of the Elk Horn saloon. It was one of the businesses that was Committee-owned and now the only saloon in town, since a mysterious fire had burned down the Red Jack two months earlier. It was situated halfway along Main's white gravel street, between Obadiah's store and the *Bent Fork Gazette*. The previous owner had died suddenly, which proved fortunate for the Committee.

Not long after the Committee had attained the saloon, they bought the Bent Fork dry goods and the freight line, but their main acquisition had been the mortgages of most of the ranchers in the valley from the Bent Fork bank. They now held the power to achieve what they had set out to do: take over the whole of Stone Creek Valley.

Seated at the table were Hiram Yates, head of the Committee and owner of the Circle Y ranch, Charlie Kemp, owner of the Lazy K, Jim Hall, owner of the J-H Connected and Eustis Lowery, who owned the L bar.

'What's the news?' asked Charlie Kemp. At fifty, he was the eldest of the four ranchers. He was a thin, almost emaciated man who stood 5 feet 10 tall. His hair was grey and his face was weathered from his years riding the range.

'The herd should be here in about a month so we need to get things moved quicker,' Hiram Yates explained, 'otherwise we'll have ten thousand head of cattle in the valley and nowhere to put them.'

'I'll have some of my boys ride over to the Crooked M and give them a hurry along,' Jim Hall informed the others. Jim was a tall, thin man who, even at forty-seven, was as tough as barbed wire.

'No, don't bother.' Yates shook his head. 'I've sent for Slade Johnson. He can take care of any issues.'

'What are we goin' to do about Stern?' asked the red-headed Lowery. 'Once we start pushin' the ranchers off their land, he's goin' to ask questions.'

'You let me worry about that,' Yates said firmly. 'I'll get it sorted out.'

'I don't know, Hiram.' Lowery hesitated at the prospect of what Yates was proposing. 'He is a lawman, do we want to ride down that trail?'

Yates' expression grew dark. 'Don't you go getting cold feet, Eustis. We all knew this was coming. Once we get him out of the way, we can have Krag made sheriff.'

Lowery thought to say more but the expression on Yates' face changed his mind. He knew better than to push the big man beyond his boundaries.

There was a knock at the door and a short man with wire-framed glasses nervously entered the room. It did not bode well to intrude upon the Committee's meetings.

'What can I do for you, Elmer?' snapped Yates as he openly showed his annoyance at the interruption.

Elmer was the Bent Fork telegraphist and from the look on his face, had news that rather excited him. 'I was on my way to the sheriff's office with this telegram but I thought you might like to know about it.'

'What is it?' Yates asked curiously.

'Chad Hunter is bein' released from Hell's Creek pen.'

An uneasy silence descended upon the room for a time before Yates reached into his pocket and dug out a few coins and passed them to Elmer. 'For your trouble.'

Elmer smiled. 'Thank you, Mr Yates.'

The telegraphist remained stationary.

'Was there something else, Elmer?' Yates asked patiently.

He shook his head. 'No, no.'

'Well don't you think you should take the message to the sheriff?'

Elmer looked down at the piece of paper in his hand. 'Yes, yes you're right.'

The men of the Committee watched him go and before they could return to business, Jim Hall asked, 'What are you goin' to do about Hunter? With him back, it might be a little harder to get his old man's ranch.'

'Could be he won't ever make it back home,' Yates smiled.

★   ★   ★

Krag knocked on the door before he entered the room. It irritated him some, but not as much as Yates' whine when

21

he didn't do it. Krag was Hiram Yates' hired gun, the man the Committee chairman called upon when things needed to get done. He was a medium-built man with a cold-hearted disposition and his eyes were the windows into that darkness. He had black hair and an unshaven face. He favoured a Colt .45 that was worn tied down low on the left side.

'You wanted to see me, Mr Yates?' Krag asked in his deep gravelly voice.

'Yes, Krag. I want you to take care of something for me.'

'Something or someone?' Krag asked sceptically.

Yates gave a half smile. 'Someone.'

'Uh huh,' the gunman grunted.

'I want you to get rid of Sheriff Stern. Do you think you can do that?'

'When?'

Yates shrugged nonchalantly. 'Whenever it's convenient, provided it is done in the next day or so.'

'Consider it done.'

'One more thing, Krag,' Yates went

on, 'once he is out of the way, you'll be sworn in as the new sheriff.'

Krag smiled coldly. 'Always wanted to be on the side of the law.'

* * *

Joe Stern was doing his rounds and thinking about how he would handle the return of Chad Hunter when the cowboy from the Lazy K found him. The sun had been down for a couple of hours and the streets, lit with lantern light every so often, were reasonably quiet. The high country night air had a cool crispness to it and without a cloud in the sky, was bound to get cooler still. As he walked along the boardwalk he checked door handles to make sure they were locked up tight. Stern heard the horse approach at a fast pace and he stepped down from the boardwalk and out in the street.

Stern held up his left hand while his right sat on the butt of his holstered six-gun. 'Hold up there, mister, what's the rush?'

The cowboy hauled back on the horse's reins so hard it almost sat like a dog. 'Sheriff, thank God. There's trouble out at the Lazy K. Rustlers hit us and killed a couple of the hands. Mr Kemp sent me to fetch you.'

'OK son,' Stern said calmly, 'give me time to get my horse and I'll be right with you.'

Both men hurried to the livery and the ranch hand waited patiently while Stern took the horse from its straw-filled stall and saddled it. Then they galloped out of town towards the Lazy K.

Once out of the town's false light, the surrounding countryside was quite visible as the large moon cast a silvery glow across it. The trail was clearly defined and they kept a good pace until about two miles out from Bent Fork where the road curved sharply around a stand of large trees, the cowboy suddenly stopped his horse. Joe Stern pulled up quickly in response and his mount almost cannoned into the back of the other horse.

'What in blazes are you doin', son?' he growled.

The cowboy remained silent as a shadow on horseback emerged from the darkened trees like a wraith.

'What's goin' on here?' There was alarm in the old sheriff's voice.

A silent void was suddenly filled with the dry triple click of a gun hammer drawn back and the night suddenly gained a sinister undertone.

'Wait. Hold on a . . . '

The gunshot broke the stillness of the night and echoed loudly through the surrounding landscape as an invisible hand punched Stern backwards from his saddle. There was a dull thud when his limp form hit the ground, which caused his chestnut mare to shy away and dive into the trees alongside the trail.

'Get the horse, damn it,' came Krag's gravelly voice through the darkness, 'you'll be needin' it to take Stern's body back to town.'

The cowboy blundered off after the horse and left Krag on the trail. He stared down at the corpse of his predecessor and smiled. He was the new sheriff of Bent Fork.

3

The big man lumbered awkwardly through the knee-deep water as he tried to outpace his pursuers. He slipped on a rock beneath the surface of the shallow creek and went down. He bit back a cry of pain as he twisted his ankle. Somewhere behind him, the hounds bayed wildly as they were urged on by their handlers.

He was wild-eyed, with a livid scar on his face and looked about frantically as he tried to find a way up the steep banks. The sound of the dogs was closer so he kept moving through the water. His only hope now was to stay wet long enough to give the hounds the slip and then he could continue with what he'd set out to do.

Killer Creel had broken out of Hell's Creek and there was no way he was going back. He'd killed two men during his escape; the doctor and the guard, Luther. He knew if he went back they would hang him. Creel felt a blinding stab of pain in his head and it forced him to stop until his vision cleared. There was still one man to kill before he was done, and Creel thought about Chad Hunter. Nothing was going to stop him.

★   ★   ★

Chad Hunter entered Stone Creek Valley from the south through a notch with steep granite sides, scarred deeply over millions of years by the harsh elements of the high country. With the money he'd been given upon his release, Hunter had been able to buy a horse which resembled a scarecrow with its bones sticking out, and had enough left over to purchase an old Remington army model six-gun that he had tucked in the front of his pants.

Hunter felt a sense of relief as he rode the rutted trail. It was good to be home. He'd missed the green of the valley, the stands of trees and the snow-capped mountains that stood guard over it all. There was a flutter of movement to his right and on top of a low cliff face, roughly two hundred yards from the trail, stood a large grey wolf, silent and watchful. He was a big old lobo the locals called Scar. He ruled over the south pass. It was his domain and the ranchers of the valley left him alone, just as he left their cattle alone.

'Hey, feller,' Hunter spoke aloud.

Hunter's gaze lingered on the wolf for a moment then noticed the beast's attention drift toward a stand of aspen near the cliff base. It grew tall and thick white trunks ramrod straight and painted with small patches of black. He strained to see what had attracted the big animal's gaze when a shot rang out and a bullet fizzed past his head. He dived from the saddle and connected solidly with the hard-packed dirt of the trail. His horse skittered away, stopped, then bolted. That left the fallen rider exposed to the bushwhacker's next shot. It came an instant after Hunter rolled and came up on one knee, the old Remington in his fist. The bullet ploughed into the ground next to him and he cut loose with his own weapon.

Two shots from the Remington thundered out as the bullets were fired into the trees where Hunter thought the bushwhacker to be. Hot on their heels, he rose to his feet, but kept low. He ran hunched over to the cover of a deadfall just off the side of the trail and dived behind it. The bushwhacker fired again and the bullet chewed splinters from the trunk of the fallen tree. Hunter rose up and fired another shot into the aspen at his hidden assailant.

As the echoes of his last shot died away, a new sound reached his ears. Hoof beats. Hunter poked his head up to look over the trunk he was sheltered behind but saw nothing. Whoever was out there had used the trees for cover as he rode over the low ridge to the right of the cliff face. There was no way that

Hunter could go after him, with his horse run off like it was. He doubted that he could have caught up with the would-be killer even with his horse, so he rose to his feet and turned in the direction that his horse had fled.

'At least you're runnin' the right way,' he conceded and then decided that once he'd caught the animal, it might be smart to avoid town for the moment and go home. It would take him across Henry Barker's range, but he was sure that the old rancher wouldn't mind. First though, he had to catch the damned horse. He bent down and picked up his Stetson from the trail where it had fallen, rammed it on his head and set off after the horse.

★ ★ ★

'You're a fair piece off the trail, saddle tramp,' the cowboy observed.

'You best turn that piece of crowbait around and head back where you came from,' ordered the cowboy's friend.

Hunter was halfway across B Bar range when the two cowhands galloped up to intercept him. Both rode bay horses and he'd never seen either of them before. They wore normal range clothes and their six-guns rode high, but there was something about the demeanour of the two that put Hunter on edge.

'What's the problem?' Hunter asked. 'Old Henry ain't never paid no mind to a man crossin' his land before.'

'That's because it ain't his land no more,' snapped the first man.

Hunter nodded. 'I been away a while, I didn't know. Who owns it now?'

'It belongs to the Committee,' he was informed crudely.

Hunter felt his ire rise a touch at the mention of the Committee's name. His time in prison had come courtesy of them and he wasn't ready to forgive yet.

'I'll be off your land shortly, another mile or so and I'll be on home range.'

The two cowhands glanced at each

other before one looked at him and said, 'Is your name Hunter?'

He nodded. 'It is.'

'Go around,' the pair ordered.

Hunter stared silently at them as they both smiled smugly, then said, 'No.'

Their faces dropped.

'What did you say?' the first man asked, perplexed.

Hunter eased back his coat flap to expose the Remington. 'I said no.'

'Well I guess we're just goin' to have to turn you around ourselves.'

The cowhand moved his horse forward but hauled back on the reins when he stared down the barrel of the gun Hunter had drawn.

'That's far enough,' Hunter snapped. 'Get down off your horses.'

'What for?' asked the man.

Hunter thumbed back the hammer.

'All right Hunter, we're doin' it,' the other hand blurted out. 'Don't shoot.'

Hunter waited for them to dismount before he ordered them to unbuckle their gun belts. Once that was done, he told both men to hook them over the saddle horns.

'Right, now step back and keep your hands pointed skywards,' Hunter snapped.

He watched as they retreated a few steps then he moved his horse into position and slapped both of their mounts on the rump. The startled horses galloped off.

Hunter stared coldly at the men. 'Now start walkin'.'

'Where?' they asked.

'I don't care, just get. If I see you behind me at all, I'll turn back and shoot the pair of you.'

The men followed their horses.

'Welcome home,' Hunter said sarcastically.

★　★　★

Krag entered the back room of the Elk Horn saloon where Yates and Jim Hall were seated at the table discussing business. Yates looked up and asked, 'Is it done?'

'Nope.' Krag shook his head. 'I missed.'

Yates froze as his ire grew. 'What do you mean, you missed?'

'He rode into the valley, I shot at him and I missed. That's what I mean.'

'God damn it, don't sass me, Krag,' Yates snapped as his anger boiled over. He jabbed a finger at the star pinned to Krag's vest. 'Remember, I can take that damn thing away from you, so show me some respect.'

Krag bit back the retort that threatened to escape from his mouth and instead asked, 'Do you want me to go back out and try again?'

Yates shook his head. 'No, no. However, tomorrow the payment is due on the Hunter ranch. Take some of the boys and go collect it.'

'And if he can't pay?' asked Krag.

Yates snorted. 'He won't be able to pay. When he can't come up with the money, he'll be forced off his land, and we can start to build the dam.'

Krag nodded. 'OK.'

'Is there anything else?'

'Yeah, I got a telegram today about some feller who escaped from Hell's Creek pen,' Krag explained.

Yates looked irritated with what he thought was a total waste of time. 'What about it?'

'The warden seems to think the feller is comin' here. He says he is more than likely after Hunter because of somethin' that happened in prison.'

Before Yates could digest the information, there was a soft knock at the door and Pam Yates (nee Holder) entered the room.

Yates smiled warmly at her. 'Pam my dear, is it that time already?'

'It is, Hiram,' she answered and returned his smile.

'Well then, if you'll excuse me, gentlemen, I have to escort my lovely wife to purchase a new dress.'

4

Killer Creel greedily shovelled more stew into his mouth. He spilled some down the front of his clothes, but didn't care. This was the best damn meal the scarfaced outlaw had eaten in a long while. He slurped some hot coffee but was careful not to scald his mouth. Creel picked up a half-eaten piece of bread and mopped up some gravy with it.

'This is some mighty fine stew, Ma'am,' Creel mumbled through the mouthful of bread.

The woman remained silent as she sat there in her red floral dress.

After he'd given the posse the slip, Creel slowly made the arduous trek towards his destination. His head still hurt, but he could live with that and it served to spur on his quest for revenge. Creel had come across the secluded cabin earlier in the day. Now he sat at the roughly-built wooden dining table, and wolfed down food like there was no tomorrow.

'Your husband sure is goin' to be sad he missed out on such a wonderful meal, Ma'am,' Creel smiled as gravy dribbled down through the stubble on his chin. He looked at the corpse on the floor. 'Yep, sure is a shame.'

After another plateful, Creel leaned back on the chair and rubbed his full stomach. 'Well, Ma'am, it's been mighty fine breakin' bread with you, but I must be goin' now, things to do. Thank you very much for your hospitality.'

He rose from the table. He was dressed in the murdered man's clothes, right down to his underwear. Around his waist was a gun belt with a Colt .45 tucked in the holster. He leaned forward and scooped up the Winchester rifle from the table. He took one final look at the woman and noticed a strand of blonde hair that had fallen across her face. He crossed to her and brushed it back into place. 'I'm sorry about all the blood on your pretty pink dress, Ma'am, but it often happens that way when you get your throat cut.'

Creel crossed to the door and opened it. He glanced back, waved and stepped outside, then closed the door behind him.

★   ★   ★

The homecoming was one of tears and slaps on the back. After an emotional hug from his mother, Hunter's father stepped forward, looked up into his son's eyes and took his hand in his iron grip.

'Welcome home son, it's good to have you back. When Sheriff Stern sent word to us that you were comin' home, well . . . ' Ira Hunter's voice trailed away.

'Yeah, Pa. I know what you mean.'

Hunter thought that his father had aged some since he'd been gone. He looked older than his fifty-five years and his medium-built frame seemed to have stooped a little, making his six-foot height seem shorter than he remembered. His face too had aged, and was furrowed with more deep lines now.

'How have you been, Pa?' Hunter asked with genuine concern.

'Things are changin' around here son,' Ira informed him, 'and not for the better either.'

Before he could elaborate any more, Allison Hunter broke into the conversation. 'Talk about it later. Give the boy time to settle in. It will be suppertime soon and Buster will be back by then. We can all sit around the table and talk like we used to before . . . before Chad went away.'

Hunter's mother turned and walked to the house; he watched her go. She'd changed too in his time 'away', as she put it. Her hair was greyer, her lined face bore an almost permanent worried expression and her eyes, which normally sparkled brightly, were dull, almost lifeless.

'What's goin' on, Pa?'

Ira slapped him on the shoulder. 'I'll tell you later, son. It can wait.'

Hunter turned a circle and looked about the ranch yard; there were subtle changes everywhere. Planks off the barn, a rail down on the corral, even the house needed a little work and then he noticed one other thing. 'Where are the hands, Pa?'

'Later, son,' he said softly, 'later.'

★   ★   ★

It was after supper when Hunter and his father sat outside on the front porch of the ranch house and talked. The sun had sunken below the high peaks of the mountains that bordered the valley and off in the distance the lonesome howl of a wolf sounded eerily through the new darkness. Both men sipped their scalding cups of coffee as the steam rose in the cool air.

'It's good to have you back, son,' Ira

41

said for the tenth time since his son's return home.

'Like I said, Pa, it's good to be back.'

There was a long, drawn-out silence before the older Hunter spoke. 'We're havin' trouble with the ranch, Chad. Money trouble.'

'How bad is it, Pa?' the younger Hunter asked.

'It's bad — we could lose the ranch. There's a payment due tomorrow but we should be able to cover that.'

'How long have you been havin' trouble with the bank?'

'Hell son, I wish it was the bank,' Ira cursed. 'It's the damned Committee that's the problem. After you left, that bastard Yates bought up most of the ranch mortgages from the bank. All nice and legal, and when the ranchers can't pay, he forecloses and kicks them off their land.'

'Is that what happened to Henry Barker?' Hunter asked.

His father looked surprised. 'How do you know about Henry?'

Hunter related the story of what had happened after he rode into the valley.

His father looked worried. 'You say someone took a shot at you? And then you had a run-in with them fellers? Why didn't you mention it earlier?'

'I didn't want to worry Ma, but that's the straight of it.'

Ira Hunter was confused. 'Why would someone want to shoot you?'

'Maybe someone doesn't want me back in the valley. I'll ride in to Bent Fork tomorrow and see Joe Stern.'

Ira Hunter grew silent at the mention of the dead sheriff's name.

Hunter noticed and asked, 'What's wrong, Pa?'

'Sheriff Stern is dead, son,' his father informed him, 'he was killed a few nights ago. They said it was rustlers who did it.'

Hunter digested what his father told him for a minute. 'So who's wearin' the badge now?'

There was disgust in Ira Hunter's voice when the name spilled out. 'Krag.'

'Who on earth would give that man a badge?' Hunter asked, bewildered. 'He ain't nothin' but a back shooter.'

'Word is he was Committee appointed.'

'Do you think they were behind Joe Stern's death?' Hunter asked.

'Don't much matter, boy,' his father stated truthfully, 'there ain't no way of provin' it.'

Hunter felt a small surge of anger. 'So once again Yates gets away with breakin' the law.'

'Now son, I told you there is no way of knowin'.'

Hunter shook his head, then asked, 'What do the Committee want with all the land? They already have heaps.'

'I don't know, Chad,' Ira answered honestly, 'but the only land they're interested in is north of town. The Committee's been tryin' to get me off of here since not long after you went to prison. And you know they got hold of the B Bar. Adam Proud and Jack Murphy are at the top of the list too.

Murphy is two payments behind and refusin' to budge. Proud they're tryin' to buy out.'

'What happened to your ranch hands, Emmett and Chuck?'

'The Committee has been tryin' everythin' to get my range,' Ira explained. 'One night in town both of 'em were beat so badly, they were laid up for a week. Once they were able to ride, they got their pay and left.'

'Can't you find anybody else?'

'No one wants to work out here, Chad, they've been warned off.'

There was more silence between the two before Ira broached a subject he'd put off since his son had arrived home. 'There is somethin' else boy, about Pam.'

Hunter's face brightened at the mention of her name. 'How has she been, Pa?'

'I guess you could say she's been doin' OK, Chad,' Ira said hesitantly. 'She went and got herself married.'

Hunter was stunned, one of the main

things that kept him going while he was in jail was the knowledge that Pam would be there waiting for him when he returned. Now it was all gone to hell.

'Who?' he asked almost inaudibly.

'Hiram Yates.'

★   ★   ★

The Hunter family rose with the sun the following morning and in the crisp morning air, they set about doing some jobs before breakfast.

The new day was bright and clear, a cloudless sky rested overhead and an eagle circled lazily above the valley floor. From the Hunter home, the view out across their part of Stone Creek Valley was stunning. The ranch house was situated on a bench at the edge of the foothills on the east side of the valley. Behind them, the land steepened and climbed steadily into the mountains. The ranch was prime grazing land; well watered with some dense strips of conifers providing all the timber they needed.

Hunter was taking his frustrations out on a pile of wood when his mother called them in for breakfast. At first he ignored her and kept on chopping, but his father came over from the corral and placed a hand on his shoulder. 'Come on, Chad, you know how your ma gets if you let good food go to waste.'

'I been thinkin', Pa, maybe we could run some horses over to Boulder and get enough money to pay the note.'

Ira patted him on the back. 'Sure son, we'll talk about it over breakfast.'

Hunter buried the axe blade into a block and followed his father inside.

5

The family were halfway through their breakfast of bacon and farm-fresh eggs when the thunder of hard-ridden horses filtered through the open window and into the dining area. Five riders on blowing horses swung into the ranch yard and halted their mounts outside the house.

'Ira Hunter,' called a deep, gravelly voice. 'Come on out and pay your money.'

Hunter looked questioningly across the round table at his father. He started to rise when Ira stopped him. 'Stay there, Chad, Krag just wants the Committee's money. I'll be fine.'

Ira Hunter rose from his chair and crossed to a sideboard. He opened a drawer and took out a roll of bills. When he disappeared outside, Hunter rose from his chair and moved quickly to where his father's Henry rifle hung on wall pegs above the fireplace. It fired a .44 calibre bullet and had polished brass side plates. It wasn't a robust rifle because of the metal tubular magazine under the 24-inch barrel. While it held fifteen cartridges, the magazine was easily dented which would cause it to jam. But this rifle was his father's pride and joy and was well looked after for its age.

Hunter found a box of .44s in a drawer of the mahogany timber sideboard and thumbed half a dozen into the magazine. He worked the lever action and jacked a round into the breech. He then crossed the room to stand beside the door.

'What are you doing, Chad?' his mother asked urgently.

Hunter waved her back and stepped through the door and out onto the front porch.

★   ★   ★

'The hell I will,' Ira Hunter blustered. 'That's all the money you're getting. Interest rate rise be damned. I ain't heard nothin' about it.'

'That's because Mr Yates decided on it this mornin' before we left,' Krag lied, 'so pay up or we'll have to move you on.'

Ira pointed to the money Krag held in his hand. 'That's it, there is no more.'

'Then we'll have to move you,' Krag mocked as he signalled a blond-haired cowboy forward.

'I'll kill any man who lays a hand on my father.' The voice cracked like a whip across the ranch yard.

Every man turned to see who had issued the warning and saw Chad Hunter come down off the porch with the cocked Henry pointed in their direction.

'Well, well,' Krag sneered, 'you might want to point that rifle somewhere else, Hunter. I could arrest you for pointin' a loaded weapon at a duly appointed officer of the law.'

Krag tapped his badge to emphasise his point.

The Henry never wavered in Hunter's grip. 'That's a right shiny badge you're hidin' behind, Krag. Did Hiram pin it on personal? Mighty convenient Joe Stern gettin' shot.'

Krag's eyes narrowed. 'Just what are you sayin'?'

'Just that it worked out well for you, and for the Committee.'

'Why you . . . '

'Here's your money, Krag.' Ira Hunter stepped forward and held out the bundle of notes. 'Take it and get gone from my land.'

Krag didn't move. 'I already told you, it ain't enough. You're shy the extra hundred for interest.'

'Tell Yates it's all he's gettin'.'

Hunter stood silent and kept an eye on the other men who rode with Krag. He knew a lot of people in the valley but these were new faces to him.

Krag shrugged his shoulders. 'Then

you'll have to move off the land, now.'

The blond cowboy moved again.

The Henry bucked in Hunter's hands and the throaty roar of the shot filled the morning air. The cowboy's hat flew from his head and cartwheeled onto the dusty ground. Hunter worked the lever and another cartridge rammed into the rifle's breech. He swung it back to cover Krag who had his hand gun half drawn.

'Pull it and I'll kill you, Krag,' Hunter said coldly.

Krag froze, an uncertain look upon his face. 'Shoot me and they'll hang you.'

Hunter nodded towards Krag's Colt. 'Self defence, you were goin' for your gun.'

There was movement at Hunter's side as his younger brother appeared with a shotgun. None of the men with Krag moved, they just sat and waited.

'Well, what's it goin' to be, Krag?' Hunter asked.

Ira moved forward and forced the

money into the sheriff's hand. 'Tell Yates and the rest of the Committee that the next payment will be the last. I intend on clearing the note and tell him that if he tries to do the same thing with the interest again I'll come to town and ram the money down his throat.'

Hunter smiled. That was the Ira he knew. Not the man who was about to give up and lose everything he'd worked for. Krag stuffed the money into his pocket and turned to Hunter. 'Smile while you can, jail bird, but this ain't over. Not by a long shot. Maybe that Creel feller will get you and it'll save us the hassle.'

'What was that?' Hunter snapped. 'What did you say?'

Krag smiled as he realised he'd hit a nerve. 'Well, well, well, it seems we are not so brave after all.'

Hunter ignored the remark. 'What about Creel, Krag?'

'Seems he busted out of the pen. Warden reckons he's got a burr under his saddle about you and could be headin' this way. Me, I hope he is and maybe you'll get what's comin' to you.'

Before Hunter could speak, Krag sawed on the reins of his horse and turned it about. 'Come on boys, let's get the hell outta here.'

The three men watched the riders spur their horses and gallop out of the yard. Once they were out of sight Ira moved to his son's side — he could see he was troubled by what Krag had said. 'What is it, Chad? Who is that feller Krag was talkin' about?'

Hunter looked at his father, the expression on his face turned serious. 'He's a killer, Pa, a stone cold killer.'

$\star \quad \star \quad \star$

Hiram Yates swore loudly and threw the money that Krag had handed him across the room. The roll of notes parted and they fluttered about like autumn leaves on the breeze. Then, gently, the bills floated to the floor.

'I knew that son of a bitch coming

back here was going to mean trouble,' Yates shoved an accusatory finger in the sheriff's direction, 'and you damn well missed him!'

'He had the drop on us, weren't much we could do,' Krag tried to explain.

'Shut up!' Yates exploded. 'I don't want excuses, I want damned results.'

The rest of the Committee remained silent as Yates' angry voice filled the back room of the Elk Horn.

'I guess I can go and see the judge about a paper to make 'em move off, you know, one of them eviction things,' Krag said hesitantly.

Yates shook his head. 'No, don't worry. We'll just move the dam site and flood them out. It won't matter much in the long run.'

★ ★ ★

While Hiram Yates vented in the Elk Horn, three men rode into town from the south. The man who rode at the

55

head of the trio sat atop a large palomino stallion. His name was Slade Johnson and he was every inch a killer.

He was thirty years old with a solid build; he had collar-length brown hair, dark eyes and a rough stubble on his tanned face. It was obvious to all that the man favoured black — black Stetson, black shirt, black vest and black jeans. About his hips hung a black leather gun belt with twin holsters. In those holsters rested two Colt .45s with ivory handles.

The other two men were Jethro Sharpe and Ringo Thomas, both gunmen in their own right but compared to Johnson, they were what one would call tenth rate.

Sharpe rode slouched in the saddle, tired after a long ride. He was a thin man in his thirties with hawk-like features and shoulder-length brown hair. Unlike Johnson, he was dressed in range clothes and wore a single holster gun-rig, which carried a Colt with walnut grips.

Ringo Thomas, on the other hand, wasn't much more than a kid with a babyish face and blond hair. His pale blue eyes were set wide apart and his smile showed erratically crooked teeth. He too wore range clothes and a tied-down Colt.

Both men rode bay horses, which looked in need of a good feed. They were a total contrast to the man who rode at their head.

The three men rode silently along the main thoroughfare of Bent Fork and drew the attention of townsfolk as they passed by. Some stopped and stared but most hurried on; to make eye contact with a killer wasn't conducive to long life.

They eased their horses to a halt beside a trough that rested outside the Elk Horn saloon and dismounted. They brushed trail dust from their clothes and climbed the boardwalk steps. Johnson pushed through the batwings and stopped. He looked about the saloon and saw a wide bar room with a mass of tables scattered throughout, most of them unoccupied.

The walls were timber panelled all around, oil paintings were hung at regular intervals, the subjects being semi-naked women. Against the left-side wall was a staircase which climbed to a landing with hand-carved balustrades. Spaced evenly around the room were wall mounted oil lamps, which lit the saloon remarkably well.

As Johnson and his companions walked across the room, their boots scuffed at the sawdust-covered floor. A couple of men looked up from their card game and followed the strangers' progress. The trio sidled up to a hardwood bar with hand carved panels that ran along its front. At its base was a brass foot-rail that also ran the full length of the bar. Johnson leant an elbow on the polished counter top and reached into his pocket for some money.

'What'll it be, gents?' asked Harvey the barkeep in his usual jovial manner.

'Whiskey,' Johnson said as he pushed the money across the counter towards the barkeep. 'Leave the bottle.'

'Sure thing gents, comin' up.'

Johnson watched Harvey as he sauntered along the bar, found a fresh bottle of red-eye and returned to the men. He placed it gently on the bar and scooped up the money. He made to walk away when Johnson stopped him.

'Lookin' for a man name of Yates,' the gunman elaborated. 'He said in his telegram we could find him here when we arrived in town.'

Harvey studied all three of the men for a brief moment and then nodded. 'Who is askin'?'

'Tell him it's Slade Johnson.'

There was a flicker of recognition in Harvey's eyes. 'Wait here for a moment.'

Without another word the barkeep turned on his heel and walked back down the length of the bar before disappearing through a door marked 'Private'.

A short time later, Harvey reappeared and returned to where Johnson and his two friends waited. 'If you walk down to the end of the bar and go through the door, you'll find Mr Yates in there.'

'Find a table,' Johnson told Sharpe and Ringo. 'I'll be back shortly.'

Harvey watched as the man in black did as he'd been told and disappeared through the door and into the back room.

★　★　★

When Johnson entered the room he found five men. Four sat around a table with shot glasses in front of them and a bottle of good whiskey in the centre. The other man stood off to the side and the gunman took a second glance at the badge pinned to his chest.

Yates saw the man in black do a double-take and tried to reassure him. 'Don't worry about him, Johnson, he's mine.'

Slade shifted his gaze to the fat man seated at the table with the others. 'Are you Yates?'

Yates smiled. 'I am.'

'I came as soon as I got your wire,' Johnson explained.

'You come highly recommended, Johnson, but not cheap.'

The man in black shrugged his shoulders. 'You get what you pay for.'

'Do you have a problem with following orders?' Yates queried.

'Nope.'

Yates nodded and then introduced the men in the room one at a time.

'Now,' said the big man as he pointed to an empty chair against the wall, 'let's get down to business. I was informed your fee is five thousand dollars. I consider that to be a little steep, especially when I don't know the man I'm hiring.'

Johnson stood without saying a word and walked toward the door. The Committee men swapped glances.

'Where are you going?' asked a

confused Hiram Yates.

Johnson faced him and explained, 'Yates, if you don't want to pay the goin' rate just say so and I'll be on my way. But just so's you know, the price is for three men. And another thing, most, if not all people who hire me want things done outside the law so they hire me to do the dirty work. Now I don't mind doin' it, but you pay the money or I walk out the door. So what's it goin' to be?'

Yates was taken aback for a moment. He sure as hell wasn't used to being spoken to in this way, especially not by someone who would be working for him. His stare hardened and he thought for a moment before he opened his mouth to speak. 'All right, we'll pay the money, but we expect results.'

'You'll get 'em, don't you worry about that. Pay the five grand and you'll get all the results you want.'

6

'I don't see why I should have to move into town,' Allison Hunter protested as Ira helped her up onto the buckboard. 'This is my home. This is where I belong.'

'Calm down, Allison,' her husband said as he tried to soothe her anger. 'It's for the best.'

She looked down angrily at her husband from where she was seated. 'What a load of horse . . . '

'Ma!' Hunter cut her off as he heaved another bag in the back. 'You're goin' and that's final. Yates and the rest of the Committee won't take lightly what we did this mornin'. They'll be back and I don't want you home alone if Creel comes here after me — he's a bad man, Ma, a real bad man.'

Allison Hunter remained silent; she knew they were right.

'Here, Chad.' Hunter looked at his brother Buster, who held out a gun belt with a Colt Peacemaker tucked into the holster. The Colt had polished walnut grips. He looked across at his father and noticed the old man watching him. Ira never liked that gun, even less so after he'd killed the man in the Red Jack saloon with it.

'Go ahead, Chad, put it on. I have a feelin' you're goin' to need it before this trouble is over.'

Hunter took the rig from his brother and strapped it on. The weight felt a little strange but he knew it wouldn't be long before he adjusted to it. He drew the Peacemaker and opened the loading gate. He spun the cylinder to make sure it was clean. Next he checked the action and was not surprised to find that it was as smooth as he remembered it to be. Hunter loaded it and dropped the gun back into its holster.

'All right,' said Ira Hunter, 'let's go to town.'

Bent Fork hadn't changed much. A little, for sure, but not much. As Hunter rode along the main street he took in the subtle changes. He noticed the Red Jack was gone and had been replaced by a mercantile; he noticed the Elk Horn had new proprietors and the Bent Fork freight company was now known as The Cattleman's Freight and Storage. As he followed the buckboard on his buckskin mare, they passed the sheriff's office. Outside on the boardwalk stood Krag and he watched them pass with an open look of disdain. Hunter touched the brim of his hat and kept riding; there was no way he was going to let Krag buffalo him so he might as well get the point from the start.

The Hunter family hadn't travelled much further when he saw her. Pam was still as beautiful as he remembered her to be. She wore a pale green dress that hugged her slim frame in all the right places and her long black hair cascaded down over her shoulders.

She looked up at him and caught Hunter staring. His breath caught as he thought he saw a faint smile on her lips. He felt the still raw feelings start to stir and then he remembered; Pam was married to Hiram Yates. Hunter averted his gaze and rode on.

The Hunters stopped outside of the Bent Fork boarding house that was run by Cramer and Elsie Collins. They were an elderly couple who were now into their twilight days and had run the boarding house for the last ten years. They welcomed Allison Hunter with open arms and told her she could have her pick of the rooms.

'Hello Chad boy, I heard you were back. News travels fast around here you know.' Cramer stuck out his hand and Hunter took his firm grip. 'Never did believe what they said about you son, a damned injustice if ever there was one.'

'Thanks Mr Collins, appreciate it.'

Collins waved the thanks away.

'Think nothin' of it, boy. Now, when are you goin' to shoot that Yates feller?'

'Cramer!' Elsie exclaimed, the horror of the question visible on her face.

'Be quiet, woman,' Cramer growled at his wife. 'He needs shootin' and you damn well know it.'

Hunter smiled to himself as the elderly couple traded digs back and forth until Elsie came up to him and placed a hand on his arm. She craned her neck to look up at the tall man. 'You pay that old fool no mind, stay out of trouble and look after your ma.'

Hunter patted her on the hand, glanced across at his mother and then turned his attention back to Elsie Collins. 'I'm afraid, Mrs Collins, that it might not be possible. From what I've heard there's a storm comin'. And it could very well break over Bent Fork.'

'Chad,' said Ira Hunter, 'take Buster and head over to the saloon. Have a drink — just remember the Committee owns the Elk Horn.'

Hunter nodded. 'OK Pa, and don't worry, I don't want any trouble.'

★ ★ ★

Silence blanketed the saloon when Hunter and his brother pushed through the batwing doors. He was watched intently from the moment he entered, until he stood up to the bar to order a drink.

'I can't serve you, Chad,' Harvey notified Hunter. 'Mr Yates said I weren't to serve any of you, your pa included.'

Hunter looked around the room and saw that every eye in the place was cast in his direction. They were waiting to see what he would do. The old Chad Hunter would push the issue; the old Chad Hunter would fight back. But this was not the old Chad Hunter. In prison he'd acquired a sixth sense for trouble and as he cast his gaze over the crowd he noticed the three gunmen. Two were dressed like normal range hands but the other one, the man in black, Hunter had him marked as Yates' trouble-shooter and if he started anything in the saloon, he figured he would have to go up against him. That was something he wanted to avoid because Buster was with him.

'All we want is a drink, Harvey,' Buster protested. 'It ain't right.'

'Sorry, Buster, it ain't goin' to happen.'

Hunter placed a hand on his brother's shoulder. 'Come on Buster, let's go.'

Buster couldn't believe what he was hearing. 'What do you mean, go? Are you just goin' to take it?'

'Yeah, I'm just goin' to take it,' Hunter confirmed.

Before Buster could say more, the crowd parted and the large form of Hiram Yates waded through.

'Look who's home from the pen.' He faked a broad smile. 'If it isn't the jail bird himself.'

Hunter straightened up and faced

Yates square on. 'Hello Hiram, got a little bigger I see.'

The big man ignored the barb. 'I heard the sheriff had a little trouble out your way today collecting payment. Tell your pa not to worry about it. I'll waive the interest. What he paid will be fine.'

Hunter eyed him suspiciously. 'That's mighty generous of you, Hiram. But the next time you want a payment, come get it yourself. Because if Krag puts a foot on our range again I might just forget he's wearin' a badge. And one more thing, don't push our family anymore. You do and I'm goin' to push back, hard.'

The two men eyed each other coldly and Hunter could see that Yates was not happy with the way he'd been spoken to.

Hunter moved to leave when Yates stopped him. 'Hold up, Chad, I've someone for you to meet.'

Yates waved to the man in black, who came to stand beside him. He noticed the other two men shift in their chairs.

'This is Slade Johnson, he works for me.' Yates paused to see if Hunter knew the name. When he said nothing the fat man continued, 'The next time I need payment or anything from your family, I'll send him.'

'You do that,' Hunter acknowledged and turned his back on Yates and his hired gun. He pushed the protesting Buster along in front and made for the batwings.

'That was easy,' Johnson smiled.

Yates nodded grimly. 'Yeah, too easy. He's not normally one to give up without a fight. He could be up to something so keep an eye on him.'

'Sure, no problem.'

Meanwhile, outside on the boardwalk Buster was still berating his older brother. 'What was that? Have you turned yeller all of a sudden?'

Hunter snapped and grabbed his brother by the collar of his red cotton shirt. With strength driven by pent-up rage, he threw his brother from the boardwalk out into the street. People stopped and stared at the spectacle. Hunter followed Buster, dragged him to his feet and saw the look of fear on the younger Hunter's face.

'Listen to me, Buster, and listen good.' There was fire in his eyes that burned bright. 'That feller in there, the one dressed in black, is a professional gun OK, but what you failed to see, if you were takin' any notice, were his two friends. It would have been suicide to do anythin', so don't ever again call me yeller. I just saved both of our lives.'

Hunter whirled about and stalked angrily off, leaving his brother standing open-mouthed.

★   ★   ★

'A little harsh on him, weren't you?' asked a melodic voice as Hunter passed by the Bent Fork drapery.

He stopped and looked up at Pam who stood above him on the boardwalk. He stared at her, not saying a word, and just took in her beauty.

'That's twice today, Chad.'

He looked confused. 'Twice what?'

'Twice I've seen you stare at me with that same look in your eyes.'

'It's a little hard not to,' he said honestly.

'Have you got time for a coffee or a talk over at the café?'

He shook his head. 'It wouldn't be right for you to be seen with me. Not now you're married to Yates.'

'I'd like to explain if you would let me,' Pam tried to change his mind.

'Nope, it would be a waste of time,' Hunter replied. 'I still wouldn't understand why you would marry the man who sent me to jail.'

There was hurt in her eyes and Hunter cursed himself inwardly for putting it there. He thought about saying something to try and make it go away but there was nothing; she'd married the man who'd put him in prison and he would never understand why. Hunter turned away and left her standing there, the hurt still in her eyes.

7

Killer Creel entered Stone Creek Valley late in the afternoon and made camp well off the trail, deep in a stand of spruce. The horse he'd taken from the murdered couple at the cabin was tied to a low-hanging branch. He built a small fire and sat down to eat some of the leftover food he'd taken from the cabin.

As he chewed, he mulled over the fact that he had finally reached the valley of the man he was after; the man he had come here to kill and nothing was going to stop that.

The sun sank slowly behind the snow-covered rocky mountain peaks and a black shroud descended upon the land. A cool chill bit at Creel's exposed skin as a light breeze drifted through the trees. The outlaw watched as the orange flames licked at the air above them, fed by the dry sticks he had gathered just before dark.

A sharp, stabbing pain in his head brought him out of his daze and he raised his hand to the area it emanated from. His vision blurred and he blinked several times to try and clear it. The pain intensified and Creel gasped out loud as he began to feel like his head would burst. Then as fast as it came, the pain went. Creel blinked his eyes to clear them of the tears that had formed. And then he saw them. The amber coloured orbs that seemed to hang in mid-air, across from him on the other side of the fire.

Creel froze as a low guttural growl reached out to him across the flames. A cold chill ran down his spine as he realised he was as close to death now as he had ever been. Slowly, Creel moved his hand towards the Colt at his hip. The growl grew louder and the outlaw stayed his hand for a brief moment before he moved it again.

Slowly. No sudden moves. Just nice

and slow. The wolf's low growl now became a loud snarl as it leapt across the flames and hit Creel square in the chest, its snapping jaws lunging for his exposed throat.

*   *   *

Across the Stone Creek Valley, on the other side of Bent Fork, was the Circle P ranch, owned by Adam Proud. He lived there with his wife Amelia and their daughter of twenty-one years, Emma. Proud was just that, a proud man. He'd come to the valley with his family and started from scratch to build his ranch up to what it was. He was now in his fifties, as was Amelia; the Committee was threatening to take away everything that he had worked for.

They'd made offers on the ranch, not enough money by any means, but the offers were there. Gradually they became less and Proud was warned that the Committee was growing impatient and that he needed to think seriously about what might happen if he kept refusing.

Proud had just climbed into bed when both he and Amelia heard the approach of horses. It started out as a low drumming sound but soon grew into a cacophony of hoofs as the horses and their riders thundered into the yard.

'What's going on?' Amelia asked and Proud could hear the fear in his wife's voice.

'I don't know,' he said as he climbed back out of bed. 'Wait here.'

Proud pulled on a pair of denim pants and a long sleeved shirt and hurried through the darkened ranch house. When he reached the front door he paused to listen. Outside, he could hear faint voices and recognised one as Hennessy, who was one of his longer-serving ranch hands. He was sure the other two hands would be out there as well but he couldn't make out their voices.

Before he opened the door, Proud

reached up above it where a Winchester rifle hung on two pegs. He took it down and jacked a round into the breach, then opened the door and stepped outside into the pale moonlight. There were five riders in all. Hiram Yates, Krag, Slade Johnson, Jethro Sharpe and Ringo Thomas. They were still sitting saddle and Krag was the one talking to Hennessy.

'Just get your boss out here now,' Krag ordered. 'Wake him the hell up if you have to.'

'That won't be necessary,' snapped Proud as he stepped out into the yard. 'I'm right here, now what do you want that can't wait until the sun comes up?'

Hiram Yates moved his big grey horse forward. Its coat seemed to shimmer in the silver moonlight.

'I've come for your answer, Proud.' It was more a demand than a request. 'But before you do answer, think about this. Either way you are leaving here tonight. With money or without.'

Proud felt his anger rise at the

ultimatum Yates had given him. 'Is it the same offer as last time, Yates?'

The fat man nodded stiffly. 'It is.'

'Then you go to hell,' the rancher snarled.

It seemed as if a great calmness had come over Yates, a resignation that this was what he had expected from the rancher who stood in front of him. Then he spoke slowly and clearly. 'Sheriff, I do believe Proud has a rifle and intends to use it.'

Before Adam Proud could say anything else, the yard filled with the roar of six-guns. The rancher was knocked back by two bullets from Johnson's pearl-handled Colts. Proud dropped the rifle he'd been holding and his arms flailed wildly before he thudded in the dirt and became still.

An open-mouthed Hennessy stared at the unmoving form of his boss. The coldness of the killing kept him immobile for a brief moment before he started to react. It was all too late because Johnson had now turned his guns and shot him down just as callously as he'd done Proud.

By now Krag and the other two gunmen had drawn their weapons and their guns joined in the song of death. The remaining two cowhands died in the dirt just as the others had done.

There was a wild shriek from the ranch house. The door flew open and out rushed the two Proud women, dressed in their white nightgowns. Hiram Yates watched as they knelt beside Adam Proud's prone form and tried in vain to wake him from his eternal sleep.

Amelia Proud looked up at the man who sat atop the grey and with tears made invisible by the darkness, cried out defiantly, 'You damned murderer, Hiram Yates! May the devil take your soul to hell!'

'You were warned,' Yates said callously. 'I'll give you a day or so to get things organised and then you get off my land.'

'This is our land,' she hissed, 'and

we'll not be moved off it.'

Yates' eyes narrowed. 'You will be gone by the time I come back in two days. If you are not, then you'll be buried next to the men.'

The five riders turned their horses and rode out of the ranch yard, leaving the two wailing women behind them.

* * *

The news of Adam Proud's murder spread through the valley like a raging wild fire. Up to a point, it had the intended effect that over the next few days, two other families would pack up and leave their livelihoods behind in fear of what would happen to them. When the news reached the Hunter ranch, Ira and Chad rode over to the Circle P to help out, only to find the freshly dug graves and the bulk of the Prouds' belongings loaded onto the ranch wagon.

Both women were tired and still distraught at what had happened.

'What are you going to do?' Ira asked Amelia Proud.

She shook her head. 'I have no idea . . . go to town. After that I don't know, this was our home. Now we have nothing.'

Anger surged through Hunter as the tears slid down her cheeks once more. Her daughter Emma moved in beside her to comfort the grieving widow.

Emma's blue eyes blazed as she turned her gaze to Hunter. 'Isn't there anything that can be done? Those animals murdered four men.'

Even though her long black hair was dishevelled and she looked tired, there was defiance written all over her face as she challenged them to do something. 'Well, isn't there?'

Hunter opened his mouth to say no. With the sheriff being a Committee man and the hired guns now in town, any man knew that nothing would be done about the killings. Instead he said, 'Don't you worry. Hang around town, they'll get their justice. One way or another.'

Emma Proud stared into Hunter's eyes and then nodded slightly. 'OK then, we'll stay for a while.'

Just before they left the Circle P, Ira Hunter pulled his son aside and expressed his concern. 'What the hell was that about before, boy? You can't just go sayin' stuff like that.'

'You know there's a fight comin', Pa,' Hunter pointed out to his father. 'Yates is hell bent on takin' over the valley for some reason and he's proven that he'll kill to do it if necessary. He don't care about the law. He makes his own law. The only way to stop him is to fight back.'

'Don't go doin' nothin' foolish, son,' Ira cautioned. 'When we hit town I'm goin' to wire for a marshal. Just wait and see what happens. OK?'

Hunter nodded. 'OK, Pa, we'll do it your way.'

Ira patted his son on the shoulder. 'Good boy, now let's go.'

The four Committee men were seated around the table having another one of their meetings when Elmer busted into the back room with a nervous look on his face.

'God damn it, Elmer, don't you know how to knock?' Yates snapped.

'I'm sorry, Mr Yates, but I thought you would want to know . . . ' the telegraphist blurted out.

'Know what?' Jim Hall asked, his irritation obvious.

'Ira Hunter was just in the telegraph office and asked me to send a wire to the US Marshals, requesting them to send a man to Bent Fork to investigate the killings out at the Circle P.'

Hiram Yates leaned forward in his chair and gave Elmer a look that chilled his blood. 'Did you send the message, Elmer?'

Elmer paused before he answered the question. He couldn't help it, the look he was getting scared the hell out of him. 'N-no, hell no, no sir. I didn't send it at all. But he'll be expectin' a reply.'

'Listen close, Elmer,' Yates warned the telegraphist, 'I want you to go back to your office and write out a reply. Make something up. Tell him a marshal is on the way. By the time he realises something is wrong it will be too late.'

'Sure, sure,' Elmer agreed eagerly.

'Now get out, we're busy.'

Once the telegraphist disappeared out the door, Charlie Kemp asked Yates, 'What are we goin' to do about Ira Hunter? Do we send men out to his place again to take care of the problem?'

Yates thought for a moment before he answered the thin man. 'No, we'll leave him be for the moment and start the dam construction. Once water starts getting close to his property he'll come to us.'

'What about the Crooked M?' Jim Hall asked.

'It will flood like Hunter's ranch. Leave it be.'

Eustis Lowery stood up from his chair and sighed. 'Well gentlemen, I must be getting back to my ranch. If you need me for anythin' you know where to find me.'

When the rancher stepped outside the Elk Horn, there was a commotion on the street. Lowery paused to see what the ruckus was about and instead of climbing onto his horse, he walked along the street to where the buzzing crowd stood. They were gathered around an old trapper who still roamed the Colorado high country taking furs. The man was dressed in buckskins and wore a fur cap on his head that covered his white hair. His aged face had more lines in it than a cliff face and when he spoke it sounded more like a cackle than a man's voice. The citizens of Bent Fork knew the old man as Buckskin. If he were known by another name, it had been forgotten long ago.

Buckskin was standing next to his old scrawny pack horse and draped over it was the reason for the excitement coming from all those gathered around. Hanging over the pack horse was Scar, the lobo grey wolf who stood guard at the south entrance to Stone Creek Valley.

'What happened?' asked an excited citizen.

'Did you do that?' asked another.

'What did you go and shoot him for?'

Eventually, the thorough interrogation finally got the full story from the old trapper.

He'd come across the dead wolf earlier in the day on his way through the pass. The animal had been laying not far from the trail, 'deader 'n hell' were the words Buckskin had used. He followed the wolf's back trail to the camp in the trees where he found the blackened campfire and a lot of blood. There was no sign of anything or anybody else.

'One thing is for sure,' he crowed, 'whoever did for old Scar here sure had a piece of flesh taken outta him. There was blood scattered all around that campsite. But I couldn't find no sign of him anywhere. He couldn't have gone too far though.'

'Good thing if you ask me.'

They all turned to look at Lowery, some of them with open hostility.

'Why would you say that?' asked a voice from the crowd.

'Only a matter of time before he started to take stock,' Lowery elaborated.

A murmur rippled through the crowd as they turned back toward the old trapper and his grizzly find. Soon the excitement rose again and Lowery was lost to them. The Committee man shrugged his shoulders and walked back to his horse. He untied the reins from the rough hitch rail and swung up into the saddle. Lowery cast the mob one last glance, then turned the bay with the white star on its forehead away from the Elk Horn and rode out of town.

8

Buster entered the ranch yard riding so fast that one could imagine that the hounds of hell were hot on his trail. He dragged the bay mare to a sliding stop, leapt from the saddle and ran across to the front door of the ranch house. He burst inside as he thrust the door wide. It made a loud crash as it rammed up against the wall.

'Pa, Pa!' he called frantically as he rushed into the living room.

'Whoa, boy,' Ira said as he held up his hands to calm his youngest son. 'What's the rush?'

'They're buildin' a dam on Circle P. It's goin' to flood this whole part of the valley.'

Ira remained silent; he walked across to a curtained window and looked out across the valley. It had been four days since Adam Proud's killing along with his hands, and things up until now were unusually quiet. He stood there silently for a long time.

'What are we goin' to do, Pa?' asked Hunter when his father didn't speak.

Ira turned and faced his eldest son, his expression grim but his voice held a certainty when he spoke. 'We wait for the marshals.'

Buster couldn't believe what he'd heard. 'In the meantime our land goes under water. You need to fight back, Pa. The ranchers need to band together and fight!'

The last few words were all but shouted in his frustration and Hunter stepped forward to emphasise what his father had said. 'Pa said to wait, Buster, so we wait. End of story.'

The younger Hunter stood fixed to the spot, a look of disgust on his face. He opened his mouth to say something but changed his mind and clamped it shut. Instead, he turned on his heel, stormed out and slammed the door behind himself. It wasn't long before the sound of hoof beats reached their ears.

'He's right, Pa,' Hunter allowed, 'we need to fight before it's too late and Yates takes over the whole damned valley.'

'I know, damn it,' Ira snapped, 'but I want it done legal, so we wait for the marshals. I knew Yates was up to somethin' when he didn't push the issue with the money. Now I know why. I just hope your brother doesn't do anythin' stupid beforehand.'

Hunter nodded. 'Me too. But why would Yates dam this part of the valley when his ranch is downstream of it?'

'I think the real question is, why would the Committee need so much water? With even just a small dam, it would still flood a lot of land.'

'The only thing he'd need that much water for would be a large herd of cattle. With all that water he could run thousands of beeves at this end of the valley,' Hunter surmised.

'Whatever it is,' Ira said grimly, 'he's willin' to kill to achieve it.'

★   ★   ★

The three men sat on their horses atop the low rise that looked directly over the construction area for the dam being built on Stone Creek. Work was surging ahead and Hiram Yates was more than happy with the progress. The new site for the dam had been chosen well, for where it was now situated, the valley's undulations worked in their favour. It was being built at a point where Stone Creek cut its way through a low rolling ridge that ran perpendicular to the rocky stream. All that really needed to be done was dam the gap, and the natural barrier of the ridge would do the rest. Alongside Yates were Jim Hall and Slade Johnson. The latter had become more Yates' personal body-guard of late.

'Seems to be goin' well, Hiram,' Hall observed.

A large toothy grin split the big man's face. 'It's going better than well, Jim. In a month or so they can fill some of the centre in and start the water backing up for the man-made lake. Just in time for the first herd's arrival.'

His comment caught the rancher off guard and Hall gave him a questioning look. 'What do you mean, first herd? We've never talked about another herd comin' in.'

'Jim, with all the land and water the Committee will have, we'll be able to run three times what we have coming in. Possibly more.'

It was the first time that Jim Hall had seen a glimmer of something in Hiram Yates' eyes and it made him feel uneasy. Yates was power drunk. He wanted more and it appeared that he would let nothing stop him from getting it.

'Just think about it, Jim,' the big man continued, 'everywhere you go in the valley you would be surrounded by Committee cattle. Thirty thousand of them — more! Over a million dollars' worth just roaming free.'

'It does sound good,' Hall agreed.

'Damn right it does, it's all ours for the taking and God help anyone who gets in the way.'

★ ★ ★

It was just after midnight when the low rumble of far-off thunder rolled across Stone Creek Valley, which was strange because there wasn't a cloud in the sky and the stars sparkled like diamonds as they surrounded the bright silvery moon. The rumble was soon followed by a popping sound that carried for miles through the clear night air. The sound ebbed and flowed until it eventually petered out and only the sounds of the night remained.

The rumble woke Hunter from his sleep and caused him to sit up and swing his legs over the edge of the metal framed bed. He rubbed at his eyes before he stood and padded across to his bedroom window. The moon was still up and parts of the surrounding country were made visible by the pale silver light it cast. Hunter stood and looked out the window for a while longer before he shrugged his shoulders and went back to bed. It would be morning before he found out what had happened and from then on the Stone Creek Valley war really hotted up.

★ ★ ★

The dull drumming of a fist on wood dragged Hiram Yates out of a deep slumber and into the land of the living.

'Who in the hell could that be?' he cursed aloud as he cast his covers aside and hauled his large frame out of his warm, soft bed. He reached across to his bedside table and picked up an imported Webley Bulldog pocket revolver, which was chambered for five .44 short rimfire cartridges and had an effective range of fifty feet. The whore in the other side of the large bed rolled and mumbled something incoherent

95

and went back to sleep. As Yates closed on the door, he thumbed back the hammer of the pistol; the triple click sounded loud in the dark.

Once more the hammering on the door commenced, only this time an urgent voice accompanied it. 'Mr Yates, you gotta wake up!'

Yates opened the door to find a cowhand from the Lazy K standing there with an anxious look on his face.

'What do you want?' Yates asked, annoyed at the inconvenience of being woken up so early.

'You gotta come, Mr Yates, I went to the Circle Y but they said you were here,' he said hurriedly. 'Someone blew up the dam on the Circle P.'

Yates snapped alert at the news. 'They what? How in hell did that happen?'

'Three men sneaked in and blew it with dynamite,' he explained. 'We lost two men who were guardin' it but we shot one of theirs. I think there was another feller who was hit too.'

'Hell,' Yates cursed as his anger rose sharply. 'Who were they?'

'The feller who got hisself shot was Billy Williams and we think the feller who was winged happened to be Buster Hunter.'

Yates' eyes grew hard. 'Wake up Johnson and his boys, they're in the next two rooms. Tell 'em I'll meet 'em outside the livery.'

'Sure thing,' the cowboy said and hurried along the hallway to knock on the next door along.

Yates slammed the door behind himself and moved to get dressed. Someone was going to pay for killing the men and blowing the dam. He would not be stopped.

★ ★ ★

Ira Hunter busted into his eldest son's room not long after dawn and shook him fully awake.

'Get up, Chad, we got us a problem. A bad problem.'

'What's goin' on, Pa?' Hunter asked, confused.

'Get your clothes on and come outside. Hurry, Buster's been shot.'

Before anything else could be said or asked, Ira disappeared. What on earth had his brother gotten himself into, Hunter wondered as he pulled on his clothes. Whatever it was he could be certain that it wasn't good.

Once outside, Hunter found his father with a team hitched to a wagon, struggling to get the wounded Buster into the bed of it. Hunter rushed across to help his father. When they had Buster laid out in the back of the wagon Hunter could see the large patch of red on the front of his brother's clothes.

'How did you get shot, Buster?' Hunter asked.

A wan smile split his brother's pale face. 'They're . . . they're goin' to have to . . . to start buildin' the dam again.'

Hunter shook his head and climbed into the back with Buster. 'Of all the stupid things to do. Didn't you listen to what Pa said?'

The wagon jerked as Ira got the team moving. Both men were jerked about in the back and Buster groaned with pain. Once it had settled, he said softly to his brother, 'Had to do somethin', Chad, couldn't let them just get away with it.'

'Who was with you?' Hunter asked.

'Billy and James.'

'Where are they?'

'Billy,' he paused for a moment as pain shot through his body after the wagon jolted through a rut in the trail, 'Billy's dead, they shot him. James went back to town.'

'Did they see you?' Hunter asked, concerned.

Buster gave a gentle shake of his head. 'Don't know.'

'For your sake, Buster, I hope they didn't,' Hunter warned him, 'but in any case, you've just made things a whole lot worse.'

But Buster didn't say anything because he'd passed out.

★ ★ ★

Hiram Yates tossed the splintered piece of wood into the creek and stared silently at the devastation of what had once been the beginnings of the dam. It was now just a pile of matchwood. The engineers would lose maybe a week with the clean-up before they could commence on the rebuild, but that wasn't the point. The fact that someone had dared to act against the Committee riled Yates and they had to be made an example of.

'Charlie,' Yates called over to Kemp as he kicked at a pile of wooden rubble, 'hire some extra help and put them to work felling trees in the foothills, I want this dam up yesterday.'

'Sure thing, Hiram,' Kemp acknowledged.

'And make sure those men that were killed get buried right.'

Kemp just waved his hand. Yates turned his attention to Jim Hall. 'If one of the men who did this was wounded bad enough they would need tending. Come on, we're going back to Bent Fork.'

* * *

'How is he, Doc?' Ira asked impatiently as Doctor Bernard Hayes emerged from the room where he'd been working on Buster's wound.

The old, grey medico ran a rough hand through his silver hair and breathed a heavy sigh. 'He'll be fine, may need a couple of weeks rest but he should mend right enough. I'd like to keep him here for a few days though before I let him go home.'

'Can I go and sit with him?' Allison Hunter asked.

Hayes nodded. 'He'll be out for a while, but that should be fine.'

After Allison disappeared into the room where her son was, Hayes turned his full attention to the Hunter men. 'What happened, Ira?'

The old rancher shook his head in

bewilderment. 'The fool kid and his friends blew up a dam on Circle P range the Committee were buildin'.'

If it came as a shock to Hayes he didn't show it. 'It's bad business, Ira. Why would he want to do something like that?'

'Yates is after our ranch and set on floodin' us and Jack Murphy out,' Ira explained. 'I told Buster to wait for the marshal I sent for, but it seems he didn't listen.'

'Hiram isn't going to take it lying down, Ira,' Hayes pointed out unnecessarily.

Before Ira could say any more, there was a commotion outside the doctor's and they could clearly hear raised voices.

Hunter gave a quick glance at his father and Hayes. 'Sounds like we're about to find out.'

9

Six men were about to pass through the white picket gate into the front yard of the doctor's residence when Hunter came out of the door and walked down the porch steps. He stopped at the base of them on the gravel path to block their advance. There was a distance of around twenty feet between him and them when they came to a halt. Hunter stood tall as he faced Hiram Yates, Jim Hall, Slade Johnson, Jethro Sharpe, Ringo Thomas and Krag.

'That's far enough, Yates,' Hunter ordered.

The big man smiled wickedly. 'So it is true. Get out of the way, we've come for your brother.'

Hunter held firm, his hand rested on the butt of his Peacemaker. 'Nope, you can't have him. Doc says he needs rest.'

'Buster is goin' to jail, Hunter,' Yates

spoke firmly, eyes sparkled as he was barely able to hide his glee at the situation. 'He's responsible for the deaths of two men. You know what that means, he's going to hang.'

There was movement at Hunter's side and Ira appeared holding Doc Hayes' long-barrelled twelve-gauge shotgun. 'You'll not take him anywhere, Hiram. If you do it'll be over my dead body.'

'You seem to forget,' Yates sneered, 'I have the law on my side.'

Krag stepped confidently forward. 'I'm takin' him in now, move aside.'

'Take another step and see what happens, Krag,' Hunter warned softly.

'Get out of my way, jailbird,' Krag ordered and made to push past the men in his path.

Hunter left it until Krag was almost on top of him when he brought his hand up full of Peacemaker and hit Krag a solid blow up the side of his head with its 4¾ inch barrel. Krag grunted and collapsed to the ground but the Peacemaker's arc didn't stop until it snapped into line with Hiram Yates' midriff.

'The next one who moves will get their boss's gut shot.' Hunter's challenge stayed hands as they went for holstered guns. 'Now seeing as he has such a big paunch it might be hard to miss from this distance. But if you fellers want to take that chance, have at it.'

'No — wait.' The fear was evident in the big man's voice.

Hunter levelled his cold stare at Slade Johnson. 'How about you? You want to try?'

Johnson nodded at Ira. 'Even if I did, the old man's got a scattergun. Wouldn't do me any good.'

'Just you remember that,' Ira confirmed.

'What about you, Jim?' Hunter asked the tall rancher. 'Just say the word and I'll put a bullet in your boss here and you can take over the Committee.'

There was a look of panic on Yates' face and he licked his lips nervously, but Hall remained silent.

'No?' Hunter shrugged his shoulders. 'Too bad. Looks like you get to live, Hiram.'

'He's bluffin',' Johnson said savagely.

'Maybe,' Hunter allowed, 'but the question remains. Is your boss willin' to find out if I am or not?'

Yates screwed his face up into a mask of hatred. He was being made a fool of and he didn't like it one bit. On the other hand he didn't relish dying either. 'This isn't over by a long shot, Hunter.'

'Just haul freight, Yates,' Hunter snapped, 'before my finger twitches and my Colt accidentally goes off.'

There was a moan at Hunter's feet as Krag started to regain his senses. 'And take your trash with you.'

He watched them closely as they helped Krag to his feet and left. Once they were gone, he holstered his Peacemaker and turned to his father. 'If Buster wasn't laid up wounded I'd go in there and bust him in the mouth. All he's done is make the situation worse and it won't be long until more killin' becomes inevitable. I just hope it's them and not us.'

★ ★ ★

'God damn son of a bitch!' Hiram Yates raged and threw the wooden chair across the small back room of the Elk Horn. 'How dare he humiliate me like that? He will pay for that, by God he'll pay.'

Yates' face was blood-red and a vein stood out on his forehead. More than once, the men in the room thought surely something would bust as he stamped about the room and vented loudly.

'Do you want I should go back and kill him for you?' Johnson asked casually.

The big man's eyes snapped to the gunfighter. 'No. I want him alive so I can hurt him some before he dies. He will learn that there are consequences to humiliating me.'

'What do you plan on doin' then?' Krag asked and then winced as Ruby, one of the whores who worked in the Elk Horn, dabbed too hard at the open wound in his scalp where Hunter's gun had opened it up.

Hiram Yates smiled coldly. 'Listen up and I'll tell you.'

*   *   *

Hunter had his eyes closed and was dozing when he heard her voice in the other room. He sat up in the padded lounge chair, which was in a corner of Doc Hayes' darkened living room. He thought there was a hint of urgency to the voice as the tones fought their way into the room from behind the closed door. Hunter looked towards the mantle that sat over the blackened hole that was an open fireplace. Sitting on it was a wooden clock and he could just make out that the time was a little after three.

Hunter climbed to his feet and walked hesitantly towards the door. He rested his hand on the knob and paused, listened and worked out that the other voice was his father's. When he turned the knob and swung the door open, there she was. Pam never failed to take his breath away every time he laid eyes on her.

She wore a light blue dress that fell almost to the ground in length, with puffed sleeves and a form-fitting bodice. His heart pounded as she turned and looked at him. Pam smiled warmly, but only briefly. It was enough to make Hunter's memories of what they once shared flood back.

'Good, you're awake,' Ira said, then explained, 'I was about to come and wake you up.'

'What's the matter?'

'Pam was just saying that Yates is going to send men out to the ranch tonight and burn it.'

Hunter looked at her sceptically. 'And you believe her?'

'Why would she lie?' Ira asked his son.

Hunter shrugged and sarcasm dripped from his next words. 'Why not? After all she is married to the man who wants our range. Or did that not occur to you?'

'Now wait just a minute Chad,' Ira cautioned, 'there are things at play here that you know nothing about.'

'Don't bother, Ira,' Pam snapped and Hunter saw the fire in her eyes that replaced the hurt. 'I feel you would be wasting your breath, just as I have. Now that I have said what I came to say, I'll be going.'

They watched her leave and then the older Hunter whirled around on his son. 'By hell, boy, I ought to take you outside and whip some sense into that lame brain of yours.'

Hunter was surprised at the anger his father exhibited. 'What for? She was the one who went and married Yates. What does she expect? Me to sit back and be all right with it? And then she turns up here with some story about the Committee goin' to burn our home to the ground. The very Committee that her husband is in charge of. Are we meant to believe that?'

'Like I said, son,' Ira explained in a low, firm voice, 'there are things here that you know nothing about. Your mother and I were sworn to secrecy by that girl because she thought it better that way.'

'Like what?'

'Nope,' the old rancher shook his head, 'that's somethin' you'll have to find out from her. If she'll talk to you now after that little fuss you kicked up. Somehow I doubt it, but who knows.'

Hunter felt like a scolded child, but after what his father had said, he knew he would have to talk to Pam. If she would talk to him, that was.

'All right, I'll go talk to her.'

'No you ain't,' Ira corrected, 'you are goin' to find yourself a horse and head out to the ranch.'

'But . . . '

'No buts about it, Chad,' his father cut him off. 'Get out there and take the Henry down from its pegs. Then find yourself a good spot where you can keep an eye on the ranch. If them sons of bitches show up, you cut loose and make 'em wish that they'd never been born. Don't mess around, Chad, if they're goin' to burn the house, you kill 'em.'

'What about you, Pa? What if they come after Buster? You'll be here on your lonesome,' Hunter pointed out.

'I'll be fine,' Ira assured him. 'Doc Hayes' shotgun will deter them if they get any ideas.'

'OK, fine, I'll go,' Hunter agreed, but he was far from convinced that it was the right thing to do.

★ ★ ★

By the time the ranch came into view the sun was low in the sky and the hard-ridden horse that he'd hired from the livery was starting to labour beneath him. It looked as though he'd reached home before the others, which was good. But as he entered the ranch yard things changed, something didn't feel right.

Hunter reined in and looked about. It was all quiet; nothing moved. But was it too quiet? The hair on the back of his neck stood on end and a prickle of anxiety ran down his back. His eyes darted left and right. Why couldn't he work it out? What could it be that made his senses jangle? And then he saw the yellowed curtain move.

The window shattered when the bullet smashed through it after the shooter on the inside opened up at Hunter. It travelled across the open area in a heartbeat and ploughed into his left side, gouged a deep furrow and knocked him from the saddle. He hit the ground hard and the air was driven from his lungs with a whoosh.

Hunter lay there stunned as the horse skittered sideways then galloped off. A burning sensation started to radiate from the wound and he could feel the wet, warm blood start to run freely. For a brief period of time Hunter couldn't move, but with the pain, movement was returning also.

The door of the ranch house creaked as it swung open and then slammed shut, footsteps clunked on the boards of the porch followed by the stomping sound of someone descending the steps. Hunter knew he had to move or he would die where he lay in the dirt. He willed himself to roll and a moan escaped his lips as pain shot through his side and took his breath away.

Need to get my gun, he thought and reached down to find it still in its holster. The fingers of his right hand wrapped around its butt and slowly, almost torturously, drew it from his holster. Hunter looked up and through blurred vision saw the figure walking towards him. He blinked a few times to clear his sight and as he did, he saw standing before him what was once Killer Creel.

The encounter with the wolf had left Creel almost unrecognisable. The old lobo had torn a hunk of flesh from the killer's throat and where once he'd had a scar on his face, now he was lucky to have a face at all. What replaced most of it was a raw, suppurating mess. Red lines of travelling infection could be seen where his shirt had been ripped open by the animal's frenzied attack. He stood over Hunter swaying. Creel was dying but sheer will power had kept him alive for this moment. He was determined to kill Hunter and that time had come.

'Are you ready to die, Hunter, you son of a bitch?' The words came out in an unintelligible jumble.

Hunter gaped at the horrific sight that stood over him. What did he say? he wondered. There was no mistaking Creel's intentions as he started to lift the handgun to bring it to bear. The only hint that the killer was smiling was a small spark in his single eye. The other was missing and the socket was an empty, pus-oozing hole.

The spark was extinguished as Hunter's Peacemaker thundered and a .45 calibre bullet blew a hole in the outlaw's chest. The first shot was followed by another that punched into the killer's middle and yet another made mush of Creel's brains as it passed through his head.

There was a dull thud as the killer's body fell to the hard-packed earth and remained still. Hunter kept the smoking Colt in his fist, pointed at the dead outlaw. When there was no movement, he was satisfied that Creel was dead.

Adrenaline coursed through his body, which masked some of the pain that was radiating from the gash in his side. He rolled over and sat up. He holstered his gun and winced with the pain as he tore the shirt open to look at the wound. It was a deep, angry looking furrow that bled freely and began to hurt like a bitch.

Hunter tried to stand, and after a couple of attempts was successful. He wobbled for a moment on unsteady feet and then decided he was right enough to take a step. His left foot shuffled forward as he took his first towards the ranch house. Then his right foot rose and fell, followed by Hunter as his head spun and the ground rose up to meet him. What followed was an all-consuming blackness that washed over him and mercifully took his pain away.

10

They came for Buster Hunter just before midnight. Hiram Yates led the group of vigilantes, which consisted of the other members of the Committee. Accompanying them were Krag and Yates' hired guns. Krag held the rope. The front door of the doctor's house was no obstacle for the tide of men who busted in and began to randomly check rooms until they found the right one. They dragged the wounded young man from his bed while he howled with the pain of his forceful removal.

'Hold it right there, Yates, you son of a bitch!' Ira Hunter ordered as he faced them with Doc Hayes' shotgun. 'Put the boy back in his bed or I'll drop you where you stand.'

Ira blocked the hallway and the only way out was past him. The men stopped where they were and Slade Johnson was the first to assess the situation.

'He won't shoot,' he ventured, 'not in here with that scattergun. There's too much chance he'll hit his son.'

Johnson was right and Ira's facade wavered for a brief moment, but it was long enough for the vigilantes to see it. The roar of the hired killer's Colt filled the hall and Ira Hunter lifted to his toes when the bullet hit him in the chest. The shock of the impact was visible in his lined face and the strength slowly ebbed from his body. He lost his grip on the gun and it thudded to the floor. Ira reached out with a hand to brace himself against the wall, only to slide down it and crumple in a heap on the floor.

'Right, get him out of here,' Yates snapped.

'What do you think you are doing?' demanded Hayes as he became the next man to block their path.

Johnson raised his gun to shoot the medico but was stopped by Yates.

'Don't shoot him!' the big man cried.

'He's the only doctor in town. Could be we'll need him before this is over.'

Slade Johnson scowled and strode forward. He raised his six-gun, brought it down on the doctor's head, and knocked him to the floor.

'Now, let's get the hell out of here,' he snarled.

They bundled Buster outside with rough hands as he pleaded weakly for his life; his pleas, however, fell on deaf ears. Buster Hunter was about to become an example of what happened if anyone blatantly opposed the Committee.

It was an example the town of Bent Fork would remember for a long time.

★   ★   ★

A gust of putrid hot air blasted into Hunter's face and brought him out of his deep sleep. The sudden motion startled the horse that stood over him and it backed away. The move also sent a wave of agony through Hunter's side and caused his wound to bleed some more.

He gasped in pain and rolled onto his back. The morning sun immediately tried to blind him and he was forced to raise an arm to block out the fierce rays. There was some confusion at first and then it all came back to him. Pam, the warning, the ride to the ranch and . . . Creel.

Hunter's eyes snapped open and he frantically looked about, oblivious to the pain he now inflicted upon himself. He clawed at his Peacemaker and drew it from the holster. Once he'd located his target he lined the gun up on the prone form that lay in the dirt. Another wave of pain swept over him but the weapon remained unmoved, just like the body of Killer Creel.

Hunter breathed a sigh of relief and then remembered why he'd gone to the ranch in the first place. The Committee were coming out to burn the ranch to the ground. Hunter looked across at the still-standing form of his home. Not the smouldering ruin it should have been if the Committee had been to burn it. Which to him could only mean one thing. Pam had lied about everything and Hunter had been right. Yates wanted him out of the way so that they could get to Buster.

He had to get back to town before it was too late. He tried to reassure himself that he would make it in time, but deep down he knew it would be to no avail. Hunter staggered to his feet and with gritted teeth set about his preparations for the return to town.

He went inside and retrieved the Henry rifle, made sure it was fully loaded then filled his jacket pocket with extra cartridges. He thought about his wound then decided to let Doc Hayes look at it when he got back to Bent Fork.

Next he caught his buckskin horse and put his saddle on it, then rounded up the hired horse from the livery. After that, he struggled to load Creel over the saddle. The effort caused his side to open more and bleed a little but once it was done, Hunter tied him on then climbed into the saddle on the buckskin. With horse and body in tow, he rode out of the ranch yard.

* * *

Hunter stared at the body of his brother as it swayed gently in the morning breeze. Pinned to his chest was a note with the word 'MURDERER' scrawled on it. They'd hanged Buster from a tree which stood three parts of the way along Main Street. A thick, gnarled branch that partly overhung the thoroughfare was what they used to loop the rope over for their ghastly task. Hunter squeezed his eyes shut as he fought down the grief and rage that threatened to boil over and consume him.

Onlookers watched as he slowly dismounted from his horse and walked out into the middle of the dusty street. Hunter drew his Peacemaker and fired three shots into the air. At the sound of the gunfire most people scattered, however some remained. These were the ones who were drawn by the hope that today might be the day the Committee would be brought down. If anyone could do it, they thought, Chad Hunter would be the one.

While he waited, Hunter ejected the spent shells from his Colt and replaced them with fresh ones. Once that was done he snapped the loading gate closed and continued his wait. It didn't take long before Hiram Yates appeared in the middle of the quickly emptying street, flanked by Slade Johnson, his men and Sheriff Krag. Close behind them were the three other members of the Committee. All carried guns.

Hunter watched them come, his hand rested on the butt of the Peacemaker. The very first thing he would do, he'd decided, was to take down Yates. He was the man responsible for his brother's death, he was sure. If they shot him after that then so be it, but at least he would know the satisfaction of making the fat bastard pay. If he got the chance, he would try for Slade next he thought, but . . . he shrugged and let his thoughts die away.

When the Committee men stopped, there was twenty feet of empty space between them and Hunter. He could clearly see the smile on Hiram Yates' face.

'I told you your brother would hang, didn't I?' Yates gloated. 'Blowing that dam killed two men and the law is the law. But you already know that, being a jail bird yourself.'

'I'm going to kill you, Yates,' Hunter told the big man.

Yates' gaze drifted to the body draped over the saddle of the horse Hunter had been leading.

'Looks like there has been another murder, Sheriff,' Hiram said to Krag as he pointed to the body. 'I guess we are going to have us another hanging.'

Krag smiled coldly. 'Be a pleasure to hang another Hunter.'

'Before you go and get too excited, the feller over the saddle is Killer Creel,' Hunter informed them. 'He was waitin' out at the ranch when I got there yesterday. Tried to kill me, and failed.'

A murmur rippled through the sparse crowd.

'Not by much, going on that red patch on your shirt,' Yates observed. 'Shame, the man could have saved us some trouble.'

Hunter was sick of the talk. His side hurt, he was angry and he wanted revenge for the cold-blooded murder of his brother. 'How about you just shut your yap, fat man, and have at it.'

Yates' face turned bright red as his anger rose. He opened his mouth to yell something when another voice brought the pending gun battle to a halt.

'Hold it right there, all of you.'

Every person on the street turned and looked at the approaching form of Judge Eldred Banks. He was dressed in a black suit with a string tie at his throat. His grey hair seemed to shine in the morning sun and the lines on his weathered face stood out more with the heavy frown that he wore. He moved directly into the firing line between Hunter and the Committee men.

He turned and faced the latter. 'Go home, Hiram, you've done enough already.'

'All we did was hang a murderer, Banks,' Yates snorted derisively, 'and we're about to do the same again. If you hadn't already noticed the body draped over that there horse.'

'It had not escaped my attention,' Banks replied, 'but neither did Hunter's explanation of how it came to be. So in my lawful opinion it was self-defence and he has no charges to answer.'

Banks turned his back on Yates and did not see the unhappy look the big man gave him. The judge moved in closer to Hunter and spoke softly to the young man.

'You need to walk away, son,' Banks told him, 'get on over to the Doc's place where you're needed.'

Hunter's face was a mask of granite as he kept his stare on Yates and his friends. 'They murdered my brother, Judge. I can't just walk away from that.'

'Yes you can, Chad,' the judge's voice hardened. 'I know what they did, but it can't be undone. What you need to do now is go be with your ma, don't let her lose a third man in her life to these killers.'

Hunter's gaze flickered from Yates to Banks. 'What do you mean?'

'They shot your pa when they took Buster, son,' the old judge explained. 'He's still alive but it could go either way.'

Hunter's hand jerked at his Peacemaker but Banks had anticipated the move and his hand prevented him from drawing the gun. Hunter's eyes burned holes into the judge but the man was unmoved.

'Go be with your ma, Chad,' he said forcefully, 'she needs you. Their time will come. I'll take care of your brother and have the horses seen to. Now turn around and go. And get that wound checked while you're at it.'

Hunter paused then nodded almost imperceptibly, turned and stalked off towards Doc Hayes' residence.

★ ★ ★

'Oh Chad!' Allison Hunter locked her son in a bear-like embrace. 'Thank God you're here. Oh my, you're bleeding.'

'It's nothing,' he dismissed her concerns. 'How's Pa doin'?'

'Doctor Hayes says he's stable at the moment, but that he might not make it.'

Hayes entered the living room. He had a white bandage around his head, a legacy from the night before. He noticed the bloody shirt and looked at Hunter. 'Get that shirt off, Chad, and I'll have a look at that wound for you.'

'It's just a scratch,' Hunter protested weakly but the grey-haired medico ignored him and walked back out of the room to retrieve his medical bag. He returned a minute later and waited as Hunter removed the bloodied shirt.

'What happened last night?' Hunter asked his mother as Hayes went to work on his side.

'They came for Buster . . . for Buster . . . ' It was all still too raw and Allison Hunter's voice trailed away, replaced by a sob.

'They busted in before midnight and dragged your brother from his bed,' Hayes took over the explanation. 'Your pa tried to stop them and he got shot for his trouble. I tried as well but that gunman of Yates' cracked me over the head with his gun. By the time I regained my senses it was too late. They threatened to shoot anyone who had a notion to cut the body down.'

Hunter felt a sharp, stinging pain in his side as Hayes began to stitch the flesh. He reflexively drew in a ragged breath as the needle was forced through his skin.

'How did you wind up with this

wound, son?' the medico asked curiously.

Hunter looked at his mother who now sat on a maroon-coloured chaise longue. 'The feller we were expectin' was out there waitin' for me to show. He was the reason we moved Ma into town.'

There was a sudden look of alarm on Allison Hunter's face.

'Don't worry, Ma, the man's dead,' Hunter elaborated. 'He ambushed me from inside the house, gave me this wound in my side. Stunned me a bit and when I regained my senses he was standing over me and about to shoot. But seemed like there was somethin' wrong with him and he was all tore up bad.'

Doc Hayes paused. 'The wolf, old Scar. The man who brought him in said whoever killed him had the hide taken off him.'

'I'd . . . ' Hunter winced as the needle and thread started its painful work again. 'I'd say so. If I didn't kill him I'm sure he would have died anyway. He was so full of poison I doubt he would have lasted another day.'

After ten more minutes Doc Hayes finished what he was doing and bandaged up the wound.

'Keep it clean and you'll be safe from infection,' he pointed out.

Hunter nodded.

'What are you going to do now, son?' Hayes asked.

He shrugged. 'Guess that depends on how things go with Pa.'

'Don't worry Chad, they don't come much tougher than your old man.'

11

Three days later, Buster Hunter was buried in the Bent Fork cemetery. It was a small, sombre affair with Hunter, Allison and Ira; the latter had improved but he sat in a chair beside his son's grave. A few townsfolk, including Pam Yates, were also present.

The cemetery itself sat on a low hill, south of the town, surrounded by a stand of aspen with their tall, straight, silvery trunks dotted with dark scars. The graveyard had mostly wooden crosses but the occasional stone marker was scattered about the grassy knoll.

Halfway through the service, Hunter saw Pam and for a brief moment their eyes met. She dabbed at hers, but his were hard and unforgiving. He waited until Reverend Walsh had finished his graveside sermon before he approached the unwelcome mourner.

'What are you doin' here?' he asked in a harsh whisper. It was an attempt not to attract too much attention and upset his parents.

She looked at him. 'It's my fault, that's why I'm here.'

'Damn right it's your fault,' Hunter agreed. 'If it weren't for you, my brother would still be alive. I just can't believe that you would agree to go along with cold blooded murder.'

Pam reeled as if she'd been slapped across the face. 'How can you say that? I would never agree to such a thing. I can't believe you would think that, Chad.'

'Yeah, well, I would not have believed you could marry Hiram Yates at one time either,' he said bluntly, 'but I guess I was wrong. I won't make the same mistake again.'

A look of horror descended on Pam's face and then she burst into wracking sobs. She gave Hunter one last look then turned and fled.

'What did you do, Chad Hunter?'

He turned toward his mother who had one of those looks on her face. The kind that, when he was a young boy and had done something wrong, would make him head for the mountains and camp out for a couple of days until she cooled down.

'It's her fault, Ma.'

'No it's not, young man,' Allison scolded him. 'Pam did what she thought was right.'

'How do you figure that out?'

'Do you really think that she would have deliberately lured you out of town just so that they could murder Buster?'

Hunter shrugged. 'There was a time when I thought she would have been incapable of it.'

'That was my thought exactly when I went to see her,' Allison explained.

Hunter cocked an eyebrow. 'You went to see her?'

His mother nodded. 'Yes. I went yesterday. I found out that Hiram made it all up for her to overhear, because he knew she would come to us about it. Especially with her past deeply embedded with ours. When she confronted him about it, he laughed at her and told her the truth.'

Hunter remained silent, slowly digesting what his mother had just told him.

'And that is why,' she continued, 'Pam is staying at the Collins'.'

Hunter lifted his gaze and caught a glimpse of Pam as she disappeared into town. He looked at his mother then glanced at his father who still sat beside the open grave. Then he looked at the open grave itself. His expression changed and he rammed the hat he'd been holding throughout the service onto his head and turned to leave.

'Where are you going?' his mother asked, concern evident in her voice.

His face hardened as he looked her square in the eye. 'Enough is enough, Ma. It's time to fight back.'

★ ★ ★

Judge Eldred Banks looked surprised when Chad Hunter opened the door to his office and strode in purposefully. 'What can I do for you, Chad?'

'I want to know what you are doing about Yates and his friends.'

The old judge shrugged his shoulders. 'Not much I can do.'

'What do you mean?' Hunter asked, mystified. 'You represent the law don't you?'

'In name only, son,' he explained. 'I haven't been the law around here since they killed the sheriff.'

'What about the marshals?' Hunter asked. 'Can't they come in?'

'Can't get word out to them. That weasel down at the telegraph office only sends what Yates wants him to. Anything else don't get sent.'

Hunter then realised why his father's wire had produced no results. 'That would explain the wire my father sent.'

'Like I said, Chad, I may represent the law, but Yates and his men, they *are* the law. I'm an old man, I can't go up against them by myself.'

'Tell me something, Judge, do you honestly think I rustled those cattle they said I did?'

The old man shook his head. 'Hell son, I knew from the outset you never took them cows. You may have been a bit on the wild side but you were no cow thief.'

'So why on earth did you send me to Hell's Creek pen?' Hunter asked.

'I had no choice, Chad,' he explained. 'You were found guilty and that was it. So I was obliged to do what I did.'

Hunter nodded, the judge was right. 'If someone other than Krag was wearin' the sheriff's badge, someone honest I mean, would that help you out?'

'It would go a long way,' Banks allowed, 'but there would still be Yates' hired guns to contend with.'

'What about me?'

Banks looked at Hunter questioningly. 'What about you?'

'You still represent the law, right?'

'We already established that, not that I carry much weight.'

'Well, you can swear me in as sheriff of Bent Fork,' Hunter explained.

Eldred Banks frowned. He thought long and hard before he spoke. 'Are you sure it's something you want to do, Chad? After all your family has been through?'

'They have to be stopped,' he said grimly, 'or more people are goin' to die.'

'Yes, but it would be a fair chance the one that ends up dead could be you,' Banks warned. 'What would that do to your ma and pa?'

Hunter was under no illusion of what could happen to him. However, these men were responsible for the death of his brother, had almost killed his father and more than likely murdered the previous sheriff, Joe Stern. It could not continue.

'I guess I'd better make sure I don't wind up dead then.'

Banks could see by the look in Hunter's eyes that he was never going to change his mind. He sighed. 'All right then, if you want the job I'll swear you in.'

Hunter turned and started to walk out, catching the judge off guard. 'Where are you going?'

'A sheriff needs a badge,' he called over his shoulder, 'and I'm goin' to get it. Swear me in when I get back.'

As Banks watched him disappear out the door, he thought that Hunter might actually be the man that Bent Fork needed to wrestle it from the grasp of the Committee men and Hiram Yates.

★　★　★

'What the hell do you want, Hunter?' Krag asked, astonished to see him in the jail.

The Committee's sheriff was not alone. Ringo Thomas was propped against a wall rolling a smoke and was about to lick the rice paper to get a good seal. He froze, then dropped it to the floor.

Hunter pointed at the star on Krag's chest. 'I've come for that.'

Krag smiled coldly and tugged at the sheriff's badge he wore. 'Is this what you mean?'

Hunter nodded.

'I don't think so,' Krag said and shook his head.

'Hand it over, Krag,' Hunter demanded. 'You're lookin' at the new sheriff of Bent Fork.'

Krag's gaze drifted across to Thomas and a small, unspoken message passed between them before the outlaw sheriff looked back at Hunter and sneered, 'If you want it, you'll have to take it.'

Hunter expected what came next. At the end of Krag's sentence, Ringo Thomas made his move. His hand dove for his six-gun and had it out in the blink of an eye, hammer cocked and ready to fire. Hunter was no slouch; his draw was smooth and fluid and quicker than lightning.

The bullet from his Peacemaker hammered into Thomas' chest and the gunman went down in a flailing mass of arms and legs. His gun remained unfired as it clattered to the dusty wooden floor. With the gunfighter out of the fight, Hunter swivelled and centred his gun on Krag, who attempted to bring his Colt into line.

The room echoed with the thunder of a gunshot one more time. The bullet smashed Krag's gun arm halfway between shoulder and elbow. His arm went numb, the pistol fell from his grasp and Krag started to howl with pain as realisation hit him.

Hunter strode quickly forward and clipped the wailing outlaw on the jaw with his left fist, which caused Krag to become abruptly silent as he fell unconscious to the floor. Hunter headed to the gun cabinet and removed a sawed-off shotgun. He broke it open only to find it empty.

There were some shouts of alarm from outside as the town began to stir with the sound of the shots. Hunter hurried across to a battered desk covered with papers. He tugged open a drawer and sifted through the contents. He slammed it shut and moved to the drawer on the left and did the same thing. This time his efforts were rewarded and he found some loose shotgun shells. He fed two into the empty barrels and turned to face the door.

Just in time. The door burst open and Hiram Yates rushed in, followed by Slade Johnson, Jethro Sharpe and Jim Hall. All four men stopped in their tracks when confronted by the gaping maw of the cut-off twin barrels.

'Can I do somethin' for you gents?' Hunter asked casually.

Yates looked about the room and saw the two downed men. He signalled Jim Hall to check them out.

'What the hell do you think you are doing, Hunter?' Yates snarled.

'I'm takin' over as Bent Fork's sheriff,' he informed the red-faced Yates as he indicated the immobile form of Krag. 'You might say your man there has been fired.'

'The hell you are!' the big man blustered.

Jim Hall finished his examination of the two downed men. 'Krag is out cold, Hiram, but just wounded, he'll live. Ringo however, is as dead as they come.'

Slade stepped forward, his face a mask of murderous rage and his hand rested threateningly on a gun butt. 'Why you son of a bitch, I'll . . . '

Hunter moved swiftly and rammed the twin muzzles of the shotgun hard into the gunslinger's midriff. A loud whoosh of air rushed from his lungs and he doubled over.

'Ever seen what one of these can do at close range, Slade?' Hunter rasped. 'It ain't pretty. Plaster your guts all over the room, so I'll give you some advice. Keep your hand away from your gun. If you don't, I'll kill you.'

Hunter gave him a shove backwards

and Slade straightened up, still gasping and with a killer look that said the issues between them were far from over.

Hunter turned back to Yates. 'It all stops now, Hiram, no one else needs to die. All you need to do is leave town. Pack all your things up and go. And take all your friends with you.'

Yates snorted derisively. 'You must be joking — I'll not walk away from all that I've built. I have too much invested in the valley, in the town, to leave now.'

Hunter nodded, just what he expected. 'So be it, but ask yourself, is it worth your life?'

He let the question hang before he continued. 'Another thing, leave Pam alone. She deserves better than a lyin', cheatin' murderer like you.'

'You'll not tell me what to do with my wife, damn you.' Yates' voice trembled as his anger reached boiling point.

'The way things are goin' in Bent Fork, she'll soon be your widow,' Hunter told the quaking fat man. 'Now pick up your man and get the hell out of my jail.'

Slade and Jethro Sharpe picked up the body of Ringo and carried him out the door, while Jim Hall moved to pick up Krag.

'Not him.' Hunter's words made the tall man stop and look at him questioningly. 'He's stayin'. Drag him into one of the cells and then get.'

'What are you locking him up for?' queried Yates.

'I'm goin' to sit him in that cage for a while and let him sweat,' Hunter explained, 'and then when he's ready, I'm goin' to offer him a deal. I let him ride outta here for testimony in court that will see all of you locked up or stretch rope.'

It was after that final statement that the anger drained from Hiram Yates' face and was replaced by genuine concern. Krag knew too much and could not be allowed to talk.

'Come on, Jim,' Hiram Yates snapped, 'let's go.'

'What about Krag?'

'Leave him there,' the big man said flatly, 'he won't talk. This ain't over, Hunter, not by a long shot.'

'Don't expect it will be,' he allowed, then his voice grew cold and menacing. 'Now get the hell out.'

12

The nickel-plated badge clunked onto the judge's desk and Chad Hunter stood quietly and waited for Banks' reaction. The judge stared at it and looked up at Hunter. He smiled wryly. 'My guess is that you just opened a whole new can of worms.'

'I'm not sure about openin' one but I just gave the worms somethin' to eat.'

Banks looked quizzically at the young man but remained silent.

Hunter filled him in on what had happened over at the jail and how he had locked up Krag to use against Yates.

'He ain't going to like that, Chad,' the judge observed. 'You best watch your step.'

'Don't worry none,' he said as he patted the sawn-off he still carried. 'If they want trouble I'm happy to oblige.'

Banks scooped up the badge from his

desk top, stood and walked around the desk until he stopped in front of Hunter. 'All right then, repeat after me.'

★ ★ ★

'Oh Chad, how could you!' It was not a question that escaped Allison Hunter's lips, more a cry of despair at the predicament her only surviving son had put himself in.

'Leave the boy alone, Allison,' Ira Hunter chided, 'it has got to be done, they have to be stopped and if Eldred Banks has seen fit enough to swear him in to do the job, then let him have a run at it. Once I'm fit enough, boy, you'll be needin' a deputy to help out. Count me in.'

'Oooohhh!' Allison threw her hands in the air and stormed out of Doc Hayes' sitting room.

Hunter watched her go and he could understand her frustration. She was scared; she'd already lost one son and had almost lost her husband. Now he was going to take the Committee head on.

'Don't worry about her, son,' Ira told him, 'she'll come around. It's the only way, Chad, the only way. Like I said, I'll help you out when I'm better.'

Hunter looked at Doc Hayes and the medico read his expression.

'That won't be for some time yet, Ira,' Hayes informed him. 'By the time you're all fit and ready, I expect it'll be over.'

The old rancher looked disappointed and sat quietly. Hunter felt for his father. Ira wanted to help bring down the men who'd murdered Buster more than anything, but was laid up and felt useless for it.

'Doc, is it OK for Ma to move in here with you and Pa until this is over? I'd feel better if she weren't alone over at the boarding house,' Hunter asked Hayes.

He nodded. 'Sure, can't see a problem with that, she spends most of her time here anyway.'

'One more thing . . . ' Hunter started.

Hayes was one step ahead and cut him off. 'Sure, son, Pam too. I'll go see her and help her out.'

'If you don't mind, Doc, I'd rather do it myself.'

'You do that.'

'Chad, you watch your back out there,' Ira advised. 'When they come at you it will probably be from behind. Just remember, you won't be the first sheriff they've gone after.'

'If they come after me, Pa, it'll just make 'em easier to find.'

'I'm serious, son.'

Hunter's face grew cold and hard. 'So am I, Pa.'

★ ★ ★

Elmer looked up from his work when the door closed with a solid rattle. For a brief moment he thought the small squares of glass that comprised its window might dislodge.

'Easy on the . . . ' He stopped mid

sentence. There in front of him was Chad Hunter and pinned to his chest was a sheriff's badge.

Hunter smiled without warmth. 'You were goin' to say somethin'?'

Elmer shook his head. 'Ahh, no. No sir, not me.'

'Good, I have a job for you.'

Elmer opened his mouth, shut it and then opened it again before he asked, 'Wh . . . what job?'

'You are goin' to send a wire for me, Elmer,' Hunter explained.

Elmer nodded eagerly. 'I . . . I can do that, yes sir, no problem at all.'

'To the US Marshal's office.'

Elmer's face turned ashen as the reality of what Hunter had said sank in. His eager nod turned into a vigorous head shake. 'No, no sir, I can't do that. Mr Yates wouldn't like it if I went and did somethin' like that.'

The man was genuinely scared, Hunter could tell by the way his eyes widened when he spoke.

'You ain't got no other choice,

Elmer,' Hunter explained to the pale telegraphist. 'You're the only one who can work the key. So you do it or else.'

'Or else what?' Elmer asked warily.

Chad's Peacemaker slid smoothly from its holster and he pointed it at Elmer. He thumbed back the hammer. 'Or else I'm goin' to shoot you.'

Elmer's expression brightened a little and he pointed out the flaw in the new sheriff's plan, 'But you can't, you'll have no one to work the key.'

Hunter shifted his aim slightly so the barrel was pointed at the man's belly. 'I only said I'd shoot you, Elmer, I didn't say I would kill you. Your choice.'

Elmer swallowed hard and five minutes later, the message was sent.

'Now that wasn't too hard, was it?' Hunter mocked the still shaking man.

'Yates will kill me for that!' the telegraphist shrieked. 'You hear me? You just killed me!'

'Maybe you ought to have thought about that before you threw your lot in with him,' Hunter said as he shrugged his shoulders. He didn't care what happened to the snivelling little weasel. 'And don't forget when you run across and tell him about it to beg for your life. Make sure you do it good and he might just let you live.'

Hunter turned away from Elmer and left him there, shaking and trying to work out whether or not to report to Hiram Yates about the wire. Hunter slammed the door shut and caused the petrified man to practically jump out of his skin.

★   ★   ★

'I'm sorry, Mr Yates, but I had no choice,' the quaking man pleaded.

Slade Johnson grabbed him by his shirt collar and drove the barrel of his six-gun up under Elmer's chin. 'You want me to shoot the snivellin' son of a bitch now, Boss?'

The telegrapher wobbled on weak knees. 'No, please don't! I had no choice!'

'Not yet. Let me think.'

'We'll have to get rid of him,' Jim Hall laid out the most obvious option. 'Hunter, I mean.'

'Oh come on, not another sheriff,' Eustis Lowery remarked hesitantly.

'We can't let him live,' Hall insisted.

Yates shook his head with certainty. 'No. Eustis is right, we leave him be for the moment. Especially now that the law is coming to town.'

'Krag has to go.'

Every eye in the back room of the Elk Horn saloon turned and looked at Charlie Kemp.

'Like you said, Hiram,' Kemp explained, 'we can't touch Hunter while the law is goin' to be pokin' around, so that leaves Krag. While he's still alive and locked up, he's goin' to be a problem. If we get rid of him, our problem goes away for the time being. No other choice. The man can put a rope around all of our necks.'

Yates sat and thought quietly for a few brief moments before he nodded in agreement. 'All right then, are you prepared to do it?'

Without flinching, Kemp said, 'Why not? Just get Hunter out of the jail long enough for me to do the job.'

'I'll fix that,' Slade Johnson volunteered.

Hiram Yates knew deep down that this was the only way. 'Do it.'

'What about this weasel?' Johnson asked, indicating Elmer.

'Leave him go,' Yates said as he waved him away. 'We've got bigger problems than him to worry about.'

★   ★   ★

The sound Hunter's knuckles made on the wood-panelled door rang loud in the confines of the hallway. Although alone, he immediately looked about to see who had heard.

'Who is it?' came the soft, hesitant voice from the other side.

'It's me, Pam,' Hunter answered. 'Chad.'

There was the rattle of a key in the lock, the knob turned and the door swung open. Hunter tried to disguise the sharp intake of breath but to no avail. Pam stood before him in a white dress that fitted just right and fell all the way to the floor. Her hair hung down and framed her smiling face in a way that accentuated her beauty. Then she saw the badge.

'Oh no, Chad, it's true.' Tears welled in her eyes, which caused an ache in Hunter's chest, the knowledge that he was the cause of her upset once more.

He stood silently in the doorway as Pam dabbed at her eyes, waited until she regained her composure, then eased past her into the room.

The room itself was small with a single bed against the far wall. The bed was neatly made and had a fluffed-up pillow against a metal-framed bed head. Beside the bed was a small timber table and next to a curtained window that faced onto the street, was a small cupboard with three drawers.

'I didn't want to believe it when I heard.' Pam spoke to Hunter's back. 'But seeing you with that badge on, I guess it's true.'

He turned to face her. 'I'm not here to talk about the badge, Pam, I'm here to talk about you.'

'Why? I was under the impression you didn't want to talk to me any more.' There was a slight edge to her voice.

He didn't blame her; he'd been hard on her from the start when he'd found out about her and Yates.

'I want you to move in to Doc Hayes' place with my ma and pa,' Hunter told her firmly. 'It'll be safer there for you.'

Pam set her jaw firm. 'I'm perfectly safe here.'

'You'll be safer over at Doc Hayes'.'

'Why?' Pam asked. 'Why will I be safer?'

'Because the lid is about to blow off this whole fiasco and I want to know that you are out of the way,' Hunter explained heatedly. 'I've got Krag locked up in the jail and I aim to use him to back Hiram Yates so far into a corner that there'll be only one way out. And then I'm goin' to kill him.'

Pam saw the coldness in his eyes and paled. 'You've changed, Chad.'

'What did you expect?' he asked harshly. 'I go to prison for somethin' I did not do. I get out and find you married to the man who put me there, and on top of that the same man murders my brother. But in all that time there was one thing that did not change.'

'What was that?'

His voice softened. 'The fact that I still love you. After everything, I still love you and I want you to be safe and away from that man.'

'Oh Chad,' Pam whispered hoarsely as she moved into his arms. Their lips met and a raging hot fire flared in Hunter as the long suppressed feelings boiled over. They kissed long and passionately and when they parted both found themselves gasping for breath.

Once more tears filled Pam's eyes. 'I am so sorry for everything.'

'Not now, Pam.' He dismissed her apology. 'Tell me later. Just get your stuff together and we'll go.'

'No,' she said defiantly. 'I need to tell you why I married that evil man.'

Hunter had seen that look in her eyes before and knew that it was useless to protest. 'All right, go ahead.'

'After you were sent away to prison Hiram started coming around,' Pam explained. 'I would ignore his advances and he would go away. But then he became more insistent when he said that if I did not marry him he would kill your family, and when you were let out, he would kill you too. I couldn't let that happen. I told your father and mother out of respect. They tried to change my mind but I couldn't take the chance that he would carry out his threat.'

Hunter felt his anger build. 'Did he . . . ?'

It took a brief moment for Pam to understand the question that remained unfinished. 'Oh no, Lord no. I would not let him touch me. Although publicly, I played the normal, caring and loving wife.'

'That was why he used you to get my brother. He knew if you overheard what they were planning to do, you would come and tell someone.'

Pam bowed her head and nodded gently. 'Yes.'

Hunter placed a finger under her chin and raised her head so she looked him in the eyes.

'It's not your fault,' he said softly. 'Now get your things together and we'll go.'

13

The orange glow from the lantern cast eerie shadows across the jail walls while Hunter cleaned the guns he'd taken from the gun rack. Scattered across the scarred desk in front of him was a pulled-down Spencer carbine, which he was meticulously oiling and greasing the parts of. It was a skill taught to him by his father who was particular about maintaining clean weapons.

Hunter paused for a moment and listened. There was silence. Krag had finally stopped yelling. Although there was a closed door between himself and the cells, it did little to block out the man's threats and curses. After Doc Hayes had patched him up, the outlaw had become boisterous for a good while.

Hunter looked around the jail and decided to clean the place up once the guns were clean. It gave him something to do while he waited for the next move, which he was sure would come from Yates and the Committee.

His work was interrupted by a fist that pounded furiously on the locked jailhouse door.

He stopped what he was doing, eased his chair back and palmed up the Peacemaker. He eared back the hammer and then asked, 'Who is it?'

'It's Harvey, Chad,' the urgent voice said, 'I got me some trouble at the Elk Horn and if you don't hurry, I'm sure there's goin' to be a killin'.'

The chair scraped back as Hunter rose to his feet and scooped up the shotgun he'd already reassembled and loaded two shells into it as he hurried to the door. He turned the key and opened it to find Harvey waiting.

'What's goin' on, Harvey?' Hunter asked, not stopping.

'That Sharpe feller that rides with Johnson is causin' a ruckus and he's gone and braced young Tobias Miller,'

Harvey explained as they walked along the street. 'You know him, he's just a cowhand. He ain't no gunman. It'll just be bloody murder and I don't want that.'

'If this is some sort of trap Yates has laid out for me, Harvey, I'll shoot you first,' Hunter warned the barkeep.

'If it is, Chad, it ain't to my knowledge. I don't cotton to anythin' like that.'

When they arrived at the Elk Horn, Hunter made Harvey walk through the batwings first, just in case. When nothing happened, he cocked the hammers on the shotgun and followed him through.

Inside the saloon, Sharpe and Miller faced each other at a distance of around twenty feet. The on-lookers had cleared the immediate area and stood against walls to minimise any chance of being hit by a stray slug.

Sharpe taunted the young cowhand confidently while Tobias had fear etched all over his face. To the young man, backing down was not an option. It would make him look less of a man and that was worse. Hunter knew that the only way out for him was to tackle the gunman head on, even if it meant getting killed.

Hunter moved into position between the two men. His back to Tobias, facing Sharpe, shotgun levelled at the gunman's middle.

'Time to go, Tobias,' he said calmly. 'Get on your horse and stay out of town for a while.'

The cowhand, even though relieved for Hunter's intrusion, paused for a long moment.

'I said go Tobias, so go.'

Tobias hurried from the saloon and Hunter continued to stare at the smiling Sharpe.

'Ain't right to go stickin' your nose into other people's business, Sheriff,' he said casually. 'Might just get it cut off.'

'Do you reckon you can cut it off, Sharpe?' Hunter laid the challenge out there.

The gunman shrugged. 'Maybe. But buckin' a stacked deck ain't always a wise move.'

Hunter knew he meant the shotgun and lowered it so that the gaping twin barrels pointed at the floor. 'Is that better?'

Sharpe smiled coldly and went into a gunfighter's crouch. 'Yeah, suits me fine.'

'Hold it!' Hiram Yates' voice cut across the bar room.

Sharpe's smile turned to a scowl at the interruption. 'Let me do him for you, Mr Yates.'

'Stand down, Jethro,' Slade Johnson told his friend, 'it ain't his time yet.'

Sharpe straightened up.

Hunter looked at the man in black. 'When is my time, Slade?'

The gunfighter's eyes narrowed. 'When I say it is, Hunter.'

'All right, that's enough,' Yates cut in. 'I'll have no gun play in my saloon.'

The sound of a gunshot filtered in through the front door of the Elk

Horn. Hiram Yates smiled broadly and declared, 'That sounded like it came from your office, Sheriff, I do hope everything is all right over there.'

At that moment, Hunter knew that he'd been tricked. He'd been lured away from the jail and if he guessed right, his prisoner was now dead and with it the proof he needed for the marshals. Slowly, he backed out of the saloon. Once he felt the familiar planks of the boardwalk beneath his feet he turned and hurried towards the jail.

Hunter found the judge waiting for him in the office part of the jail.

'I heard the shot when I was passing,' Banks explained. 'I came in and found Krag dead in the cell. The killer came in through the back door.'

Hunter cursed at his oversight and said, 'I guess they were worried about him givin' them up to the marshals. Now we have nothin'.'

'How long until the marshals get here?' Banks enquired.

Hunter shrugged heavy shoulders.

'Who knows? A few days.'

'Then that is how long you have,' Banks stated.

'Have to what?'

'That is how long you have to find some solid evidence and a witness to lock them away.'

'The question is,' Hunter said flatly, 'where do I start?'

There was a knock on the door. A tall man walked into the room and greeted both men.

'I thought you might be in need of me,' said Joseph Pound, the undertaker. 'Hello Chad, things are starting to get busy now you're the new sheriff.'

'You thought right,' confirmed Banks.

'Hello Joe,' Hunter returned Pound's greeting. 'You'll find your customer back there in a cell. It's Krag.'

'Can't say I'll be sad about it,' Pound said casually. 'Anyway I'll go and see to him.'

When the undertaker was gone, Banks looked at Hunter thoughtfully and said, 'Yates and the others are taking over the valley for a reason, so I suggest that if you find out that reason then we might be able to stop whatever it is that he has planned.'

Hunter nodded in agreement and smiled without warmth. 'And I know just the place to look for that information, too.'

★   ★   ★

'Oh no.' The look of despair on Elmer's face said it all as Hunter walked into the telegraph office the following morning. 'What do you want?'

Hunter gave the panicked man his best disarming smile and said, 'Now Elmer, is that any way to greet a potential customer?'

Immediately the man was on his guard. 'Do you want to send another telegram?'

Hunter shook his head and glanced around the small but well kept premises. 'No. This time I want some information.'

Elmer held up a hand as though he were warding off an attacker. 'Uh uh, no way, you get nothing from me.'

Hunter nodded his acceptance. 'OK Elmer, that's fine, I understand.'

'Is there anything else?' the telegraphist asked warily, knowing that the sheriff had given in too easily.

'Yeah, lock up and come with me,' Hunter ordered as his face took on a stern expression.

Now Elmer was confused. 'What? Why?'

Hunter's smile was cold and devoid of emotion. 'I'm lockin' you up for withholdin' information.'

Panic now gripped the man fiercely. 'What? You can't do that.'

'I can,' Hunter told him, 'and I'm goin' to. How long do you think Yates is goin' to let you sit in jail with what you know? You *do* know what happened to my last prisoner, don't you?'

Elmer's face paled considerably at the thought of what had happened to Krag. Surely Hunter wouldn't do that to him. Lock him up and . . . 'All right, I'll tell you.'

'Why does Yates want all the land? What's he got planned?' Hunter asked the quaking man.

'Before I answer, you agree not to say you got the information from me,' Elmer said adamantly.

'Why, Elmer?'

'Yates has a herd of cattle coming in,' Elmer blurted out. 'Ten thousand of them coming up from Texas. That's why he's building the dam.'

'That's a lot of water for one herd,' Hunter frowned. 'When is it arriving?'

'I'm not sure, soon I think, but that's not all.' Elmer paused for effect. 'There are two more herds coming. Yates sent word for them. All up, the Committee are bringing in thirty thousand head.'

Hunter did the math in his head and came up with a figure that a lot of men would kill for, and then a plan started to form in his brain of a way to stop the Committee and Yates from bringing in the cattle. It would inflame the situation further but he didn't mind if they came after him. It would in fact be better. This way he wouldn't need the marshals or a rope, because he'd just kill them himself.

14

Judge Eldred Banks listened quietly to what Hunter proposed before he spoke. Hunter had arrived in the judge's office and sitting in a leather-backed chair, filled him in on the herds that were to arrive in the valley and what he wanted to do to stop them.

The plan was to get a court injunction to stop the cattle from entering the valley and cease construction of the dam while all the illegal activity of the Committee was investigated thoroughly.

'You do realise that this will put a very large target on your back, Chad?' Banks pointed out after Hunter had finished telling him what he wanted to do. 'Might as well go up into the mountains and find yourself a big old grizz. Then smack him on the butt just for fun. Could be safer.'

Hunter nodded grimly. 'I want Yates angry, Judge. That way he won't be thinkin' straight and he'll be more likely to make a mistake I can pin on him and he'll finally get what he deserves.'

'All right, I'll do it,' said Banks as he agreed to the request. 'Come back in an hour or so and I'll have the paperwork ready.'

Hunter got to his feet. 'Thanks, Judge.'

'Don't thank me for something that may get you killed,' he said seriously.

But Hunter didn't hear him because he was already out the door.

★　★　★

'Are you sure about this?' Ira asked his son, concerned that he'd not contemplated it properly.

Hunter nodded. 'Yeah Pa, I thought about it. I know I'm takin' a risk but it's the only way to take the valley back from the Committee. If things keep goin' the way they are, we'll lose our land and so will other ranchers. The marshals won't be able to do anythin' because there will be no evidence to stack up against them now that Krag has gone.'

There was a short silence, a void that was filled with the loud tick of a clock that sat on the mantle over the fireplace in the doctor's living room. Hunter continued, 'Up until now, they've used the law to get what they want, even commit murder. This way we can stop them legally, until hopefully, some evidence comes up that we can use in court.'

'You know that they ain't goin' to take it lyin' down, son,' Ira reiterated his concerns.

Hunter thought about Joe Stern. Even though there was nothing to say the Committee was responsible for his death, it was widely regarded that they had his blood on their hands.

'If anythin' happens to me, Pa, take Ma and Pam and get out. Don't wait, just go and don't look back.'

'Let me help you, Chad,' Ira volunteered.

'No, you need to take care of Ma and Pam,' Hunter was adamant. 'I don't want them fallin' into Yates' hands. You need to promise me, Pa. I can't do this if I'm worried about them. I'll only succeed in gettin' myself killed.'

'OK Chad, I promise,' Ira said quietly, 'you do what needs to be done and don't worry about anythin' else.'

★   ★   ★

It was after noon when Hunter arrived back at the office of Eldred Banks. He found the elderly judge seated at his desk, reviewing the documents he'd drawn up.

He passed them across to Hunter. 'Here you go, son, there's two documents there. One stops construction of the dam and the other stops the cattle entering the valley. The injunction against the cattle entering the valley in particular makes quite interesting reading.'

Hunter read both documents and smiled at the judge. 'Hell, that'll make Yates' day. Suspicion of Texas fever.'

'That alone will tie him and his herd up for ages. He will need to get a vet to look over the cattle before he can do anything. That will cost him time and a lot more money. Not to mention every ranch owner in the territory will want those beeves shot and burned.' Banks sounded very happy indeed.

Hunter gave Banks back one of the sheets of paper and kept the other. The judge frowned questioningly and he explained, 'I'll be back for that one. I'll start out at the dam first and stop construction out there. I want to save the best for last. If they do decide to come after me I'd rather it'd be in town than out on the range.'

Banks opened his desk drawer and put the paper inside. He closed it and said, 'Fair enough. It'll be here waiting for you when you get back.'

★　　★　　★

Hunter was surprised when he reached the dam site. Much progress had been made since the explosion that had decimated the construction site, courtesy of hard work and a solid daylight to dark shift. The workmen had cleared away all of the debris and were now well into the rebuild, with Charlie Kemp overseeing most of the work.

As he sat on his horse atop the hill, Hunter watched the men labouring, a well-oiled machine that depended upon each man to fulfil his duty. Behind the build site he observed the logging wagons as they snaked their way out of the foothills, heavily laden with logs for the work crews. He had to hand it to them; the crew knew their job.

There was a shout from down below as his presence was finally noticed and Charlie Kemp along with Jethro Sharpe came loping up the hill on their horses. They drew up in front of Hunter as if blocking any further passage.

'What do you want here, Hunter?' Kemp asked unpleasantly. 'You're trespassin'.'

Hunter ignored Kemp's question. 'Sure is magnificent range hereabouts, be a shame to see it all flooded. Mind you, those fellers down there look to be doin' a mighty fine job.'

'I asked you what you wanted,' snapped Kemp. 'Maybe you're deaf or somethin'.'

Hunter continued, a false sombreness entering his voice. 'It sure is sad to know that they'll be out of work directly.'

'Sharpe!' Kemp's snarl had the desired effect and the gunman went for his side arm.

The man's smooth draw was halted before he'd managed to get his pistol from the well-oiled leather holster. Hunter's Peacemaker was pointed at Sharpe's chest, hammer back on full cock. He smiled mirthlessly, 'Give me one good reason why I shouldn't kill you where you sit.'

'Whoa, now. Hold up Hunter,' Kemp protested, 'like I said you're trespassin' so how about tellin' me why you're out here.'

'See this badge I'm wearin', Kemp?' Hunter tapped the star pinned to his shirt. 'It gives me legal right to go where I want, when I want. So understand that from the get go.'

'Makes a purty target,' Sharpe sneered.

Hunter settled his ice-cold gaze back on the gun-fighter. A red-hot tension hung in the air between them and Kemp knew that if Sharpe pushed Hunter, the gunman would end up dead.

'Sharpe, can it,' he ordered.

The gunman smiled. 'Guess there will be another time.'

Hunter ignored the man's words and reached inside his shirt pocket. He took out a folded piece of paper and handed it to Kemp. The Committee man unfolded it and slowly read it. He looked at Hunter suspiciously and then read it again.

His eyes narrowed when next he looked at the sheriff. 'You can't do this. We need the water. Hiram ain't goin' to like this one bit.'

'Well, you tell Hiram that there ain't anythin' he can do about it.' Hunter paused as he remembered the other injunction. 'No, I'll tell him myself. Let him know when you see him I'll be by later. Tell him it's a legal matter.'

Kemp's face screwed up into a mask of rage. 'You won't get away with this Hunter, you'll see.'

'Tell 'em to stop work, Charlie,' Hunter ordered the red-faced man. 'If you don't, I will.'

With a loud curse Kemp hauled on the reins of his horse and dragged its head about and galloped down the hill towards the construction site. Before he turned and followed, Sharpe looked one last time at the Peacemaker in Hunter's hand. Then gave him another wicked grin and said, 'Just so you know, I'm goin' to kill you.'

With that, the gunman turned his

horse and spurred it savagely down the hill after Kemp.

★   ★   ★

The sun had begun its slow descent behind the line of craggy, snow-capped peaks when Charlie Kemp burst into the Elk Horn saloon in search of Hiram Yates. The evening crowd was starting to filter in and the room was already thick with tobacco smoke. He stood just inside the batwing doors and looked around for Yates. All he could see were cowboys and townsfolk, eager to part with hard-earned money.

There was a joyful scream from one of the whores at a felt covered table and she playfully slapped a man who'd pinched her ample rump. Kemp hurried across the room, pushed through to the polished hardwood bar and called out to Harvey.

'Harvey,' he yelled to be heard, 'where's Hiram?'

'He's out back.' The barkeep yelled

his answer. 'But he wanted to be left alone.'

'Too bad,' Charlie Kemp mumbled as he weaved his way through the tables to the door into the back room.

When Kemp opened the door he found Yates sitting on the back room's leather lounge with a whore called Maggie. She was a big, buxom woman with wavy black hair, a heavily painted face and a laugh that sounded like a teamster's mule. And at that point, she had her mouth firmly planted on Yates'.

Hiram pushed her away and cursed out loud, 'What the hell, Charlie? Don't you know how to knock?'

'Ain't got no time to knock. We have a problem,' the rancher informed the fat man.

Yates saw the seriousness in his eyes and said to Maggie, 'Leave us alone.'

The whore was about to protest but one look at Yates' face and she thought better of it. She stood up and left the room without a sound.

'What is it?' The look on Yates' face

was one of impatience. 'Hurry up, man, can't you see I'm busy?'

Kemp took out the folded piece of paper and gave it to Yates. The big man unfolded it and read through it, and his face changed colour as he finished each sentence. Finally, when he was finished, Yates screwed the piece of paper up into a tight ball and threw it across the room.

'Damn them!' he snarled. 'Damn them to hell!'

'It gets worse,' Kemp explained. 'Hunter's comin' here to see you after. Said it was about some legal matter.'

That interested Yates. 'What legal matter?'

Kemp shrugged hunched shoulders. 'Hell I don't know, he didn't say.'

'Have the men stopped work on the dam?' Hiram asked.

Kemp nodded. 'Yeah. I stopped 'em after he gave me that paper.'

'Well, tomorrow you put them back to work,' Yates ordered. 'All of them.'

'What about that paper?'

184

'I don't care about that, damn it,' Hiram said through gritted teeth. 'We need that dam built so we've got plenty of water for the herds when they arrive.'

'Sure thing, Hiram, I'll get it done.'

'Fine, now get the others here and we'll wait and see what else our new sheriff has in store for us.'

★ ★ ★

'The hell you are!' the words exploded from Hunter's lips as he came up out of the leather-backed chair. 'I'll do it alone. You stay right here and I'll tell you about it later.'

Eldred Banks shook his head defiantly. 'No son, I'm coming with you. I want to see the look on that son of a bitçh's face when he reads that injunction. It should be downright pleasurable.'

'And it will make you more of a target when they see you gloatin' about it,' Hunter pointed out. 'No, you stay here.'

Banks ignored Hunter's remarks and walked over to a tall cabinet with a long, narrow door he had against his office wall. He took a key from his black coat pocket and unlocked the cabinet. Banks opened the door and withdrew a sawed-off shotgun. Hunter shook his head in disbelief as the judge opened it and crossed to his desk where he took two shells from the top drawer. He fed them into the twin barrels and snapped the gun shut.

'What do you plan on doin' with that?' Hunter asked, perplexed.

'Who knows?' answered Banks. 'Might have to shoot me some buzzards.'

'Oh hell.'

★   ★   ★

When both men entered the Elk Horn it was packed with customers who were becoming rowdier as the night continued. Upon seeing the new town sheriff and the judge, who both carried shotguns, a pall of silence descended over the bar room like a heavy blanket. The crowd parted fluidly as the two men walked easily toward the door through to the back room. Halfway to the door, Hunter placed a hand on the judge's arm and they both stopped. Hunter's eyes sought out Harvey the barkeep.

'Who's with him, Harvey?' he asked.

'They're all in there, Chad,' the barkeep informed him. 'Mr Yates said to expect you.'

Hunter nodded thoughtfully.

'Care to walk through that door first, Harvey?' Hunter asked him.

The barkeep shook his head. 'Nope, don't believe I would.'

'Well guess what, Harvey, you're goin' to.'

The barkeep was taken aback. 'Aww come on Chad. You wouldn't do that to me, would you?'

'Yeah Harvey, I would.' Hunter levelled the shotgun at the barkeep and motioned for him to move. 'Let's go.'

The man paled but did as he was ordered. There was just no arguing with a loaded shotgun pointed at your head. Harvey came out from behind the bar, wiped his forehead nervously with his rag and walked to the door with Hunter and the judge close behind. The barkeep reached out and with a shaky hand, grasped the brass door handle, paused, turned it and swung the door open.

Hunter pushed the scared man through the doorway and followed him into the room. Harvey had been telling the truth. They were all there. Yates, Kemp, Hall, Lowery, Slade Johnson and Sharpe. The latter two made useless gestures towards their Colts but that's all they were, useless. The two shotguns trained in their direction made sure of that.

'You two gents unbuckle your guns and drop them at your feet,' Hunter ordered. 'I'll feel a mite better when you do.'

'What is the meaning of this?' Hiram Yates protested.

Hunter ignored him and watched the two gunfighters closely as they did what was asked. The guns housed in their holsters made dull thuds as they fell to the floorboards.

'All right, now, everyone move and stand behind Yates there.' Hunter motioned with the sawn-off he held. 'That's right, nice and steady.'

'Damn you, Hunter,' Yates snapped, 'tell me what this is about.'

Hunter pulled out the folded piece of paper he'd had in the side pocket of his denim jacket. He handed it to Banks. 'Do you want to do the honours?'

The judge plucked it from Hunter's grasp and smiled. 'Don't mind if I do.'

Banks passed the paper to Yates who unfolded it and read it slowly to take in every word. The more he read, the more his big body shook and his face turned red, then purple. His rage boiled over but not in the explosive manner that one might expect. A low rumbling voice filled with deadly menace emanated from Yates as he lifted his gaze to look at Eldred Banks.

'You cannot do this,' he said. 'By hell, I won't let you do this. I have a lot of money tied up in those cattle.'

'Consider it done,' Banks stated.

'Do you realise what you have done?' Yates snapped. 'There is over three hundred thousand dollars worth of beef in that herd. And you do this.'

He waved the paper in the air.

'Do what, Hiram?' asked Charlie Kemp.

'The good judge here has put an injunction on our cattle to stop them entering the valley,' Yates explained, his voice carrying a caustic edge. 'He says that they have Texas fever.'

'Oh, God no,' Eustis Lowery moaned.

'And that means,' Yates continued, 'we'll have every rancher in the territory wanting to shoot every head where they stand.'

'Never can be too careful with cattle you buy unseen,' Banks said cheerily.

The big man screwed up the paper, threw it at the smiling judge and snarled, 'You can keep your damned injunction.'

'You keep it, I already have a copy.'

'This won't work, you old son of a bitch,' Yates warned. 'When them cattle arrive, I'm bringing them into Stone Creek Valley.'

'If you do that, Hiram, you'll be in contempt of court and I'll have you arrested.'

'You won't be able to if you're below ground,' Yates said menacingly.

Banks' eyes widened at the obvious threat. 'What was that, Yates? Are you threatening me?'

Hiram's face took on a look of innocence. 'Just an observation, Eldred, just an observation. Never can tell when a man your age might have health problems.'

Before Banks could reply to the threat, Hunter cut in, 'Come on Judge, let's go. We done what we came here to do.'

So they left and Yates watched them go, his stare unwavering. After the door closed, he waited a few seconds before he said in a low voice, 'I want them dead. Both of them, tonight. I don't care how, just get it done.'

'Calm down, Hiram,' Lowery tried to soothe Yates' rage. 'A sheriff once is one thing, but to kill a judge and a sheriff both in one night, that is somethin' else. Especially with a US Marshal on his way.'

Yates gave Lowery a look that made the man cringe. 'It gets done tonight. You're either with us or against us, Eustis, make up your mind. But if you're against us, then I'll kill you too.'

15

Hunter was expecting them when they came. He'd been so sure of it that he'd sent his mother and Pam back to the boarding house. They'd protested at first but Hunter had insisted, and with the help of Ira, the women had finally acceded to his demands. After they'd gone, he sat in the leather-backed chair in Doc Hayes' living room and waited with the shotgun across his lap.

Ira sat in the lounge, also armed with a shotgun, while the doctor was in his bedroom. Hunter had tried to convince him to leave but he had stated that this was his home and while he still breathed, he would not be driven from it.

As bold as brass, the three men came through the front door. Jim Hall, Charlie Kemp and Jethro Sharpe were armed to the teeth and ready to kill anybody who stood in their way. There was no knock, no sneaking through a window, just a loud crash as the front door flew wide from the hefty kick given to it by Sharpe.

'I told you I'd kill you, Hunter, you son of a bitch,' Sharpe's cry rang out along the hallway as he stamped along it. 'Now I'm here to do exactly that.'

Hunter stepped through the doorway from the living room and levelled the shotgun at the advancing men. In the low orange glow cast by a wall lamp he saw the gunfighter's face pale as he realised he was only a heartbeat away from death. Sharpe lunged to his left through an open door just as the shotgun filled the hallway with a thunderous roar.

The double charge of buckshot ripped into the two ranchers who were left standing in the firing line. Jim Hall died instantly as he took most of the charge full in his chest, which turned into a bloody mess. The hallway was filled with agonised screams as the rest of the deadly hail of small lead balls hit Charlie Kemp in his right arm and the right side of his chest. He fell to the floor and writhed desperately as the burning pain started to envelope his body.

Hunter threw the empty shotgun to the floor and drew his Peacemaker. As he brought it up to waist level, Sharpe appeared in the doorway and fired two fast shots at the sheriff. He was too quick on the trigger and both were wild, one gouged out a furrow in the wall while the other flew close to Hunter's head and ended up in the doorframe behind him.

Another great roar filled the hall as Ira Hunter discharged his shotgun and pellets filled the space where Sharpe had just stood. He had ducked back inside the room and the buckshot filled the void with plaster and wooden splinters.

Ira cursed. 'Missed the bastard.'

'Goin' to have to do better'n that, old

man,' Sharpe jeered from where he was hiding.

'Stick your ugly face out again and we'll see how it fares now,' Ira called back.

Hunter moved back behind his father.

'The next time he sticks his head out, give him both barrels,' he told him, 'then I'll move forward and see if I can get him.'

Meanwhile the screams of Charlie Kemp had turned to a low moan as he struggled to cope with pain and blood loss. The light coloured floor runner that ran the length of the hallway was stained red around him as his life leaked out onto it.

'Are you ready?' Hunter asked Ira.

The old rancher nodded grimly.

Hunter leaned out through the doorway and fired two shots into the doorframe of the room where Sharpe had taken cover. He then ducked back into the room and allowed his father to take position in the doorway. Sharpe leaned into the hallway only to face a storm of lead shot, which by some miracle missed the gunfighter and instead showered his face with plaster dust and wooden splinters, blinding him temporarily and forcing him back.

Hunter moved fast and low out of the living room and into the hallway. He raced the short distance to the doorway and dived to the floor. He brought his Peacemaker up and sighted down the barrel at the gun-fighter as he fought to clear his vision.

The single-action Colt roared three times and Sharpe's chest blossomed red as he was thrown back. Hunter came up off the floor, gun cocked and stood over the unmoving body of Jethro Sharpe.

'Are you all right, son?' Ira called out.

'Yeah Pa, I'm fine,' Hunter confirmed. 'You'd best get Doc Hayes.'

While his father was gone, Hunter checked out Jim Hall. The rancher was dead. He then moved over to Charlie Kemp who was still alive but bleeding from multiple wounds. There was a disturbance and Doc Hayes appeared at his side.

'Sorry about your house, Doc,' Hunter apologised.

'Don't worry about it, son.' Hayes brushed it off. 'You can fix it for me later.'

The medico commenced work trying so save Kemp's life but it was a hopeless cause and soon after, the rancher breathed his last.

Doc Hayes straightened up and sighed loudly. 'He's gone too.'

'I can't say it bothers me none,' Ira said aloud.

'Yeah, he got what ... ' Hunter started to agree with his father when the sound of far-off gunfire filtered through the night.

All three men looked questioningly at one another and then Hunter realised what was happening. They had gone after Judge Banks too.

'Hell no,' he cursed and ran as fast as he could out the door.

* * *

'Hello Judge.'

Eldred Banks was so engrossed in his paperwork that he never heard the men come into his office until Slade Johnson spoke and startled the old man. The judge paled; he knew what they wanted. He'd convinced himself that it would be fine and that they wouldn't come after a legally appointed officer of the court and yet here they were. Yates and his hired gun.

'What . . . what do you want?' Banks tried for a brave front but stammered at the first word.

Yates smiled coldly. 'You know what we want.'

The judge nodded almost imperceptibly. 'Yes, I guess I do.'

'Well then,' the big man demanded, 'where is it? Where is the copy of the injunction?'

'Here in the top drawer of my desk,' Banks groaned and opened the drawer he'd pointed at.

As his hand dived into it, Johnson hissed. 'Be careful, old man. Make sure that the only thing comin' outta there is made of paper.'

Banks hesitated. He looked intently at the old Pocket Navy Colt that sat next to the paper he wanted. He looked at Johnson and then back at the hand gun. Decision made, his hand came up holding the piece of paper. Silently he held it out and Yates snatched it from his grasp.

Off in the distance there was the faint sound of gunfire. Yates and Slade Johnson looked at each other.

'Time we left,' the fat man announced.

A wave of relief swept over Banks when Yates spoke the words and smiled. When he realised that there was no warmth to the smile, just a coldness, a shiver went down the old man's back. The judge shifted his gaze to Slade Johnson who, instead of smiling, squeezed the trigger of his Colt, three times.

* * *

When Hunter arrived at Banks' office he found the old man laid out behind his desk, in a pool of blood that had leaked freely from the holes in his chest.

'Damn it!' Hunter exclaimed and bent down to check on the man he was certain would be dead.

Banks moaned and took Hunter by surprise. By the grace of God, he was still alive. Hunter knelt down close to the judge's face and asked softly, 'Can you hear me, Judge? Who was it?'

There was movement in the office behind Hunter and he swivelled, gun appearing in his hand.

'Whoa, son.' Ira Hunter held his hands up at shoulder level so his son could see he posed no threat. 'It's just me and the doc.'

Hayes moved in beside Hunter. 'He looks bad, I don't know how he's still breathing.'

'He was tryin' to say somethin' Doc,

201

just as you and Pa came in,' Hunter explained.

Banks murmured softly and Hayes placed his ear close to the old man's moving lips. It was a long moment before he straightened up and spoke to the Bent Fork sheriff.

'He said it was Slade Johnson who shot him. Him and Yates came here after something. He said something about a paper.'

Hunter rose quickly and rummaged through the top drawer of Banks' desk. The copy of the injunction was gone, as he knew it would be. He cursed out loud and drew his Peacemaker from its holster. He opened the loading gate and thumbed fresh cartridges into the cylinder before he snapped it shut. Then he dropped the six-gun back into its holster.

'Is he goin' to make it, Doc?' the question was more in hope than anything else.

Hayes looked at Hunter forlornly. 'I doubt it, son, I'm sorry.'

A pall of sorrow descended upon Hunter. Banks had believed in him enough to make him town sheriff and trusted in him to rescue Bent Fork and the valley from the clutches of Hiram Yates and the Committee. Now he would never see it come to fruition.

Hunter's jaw clenched. The hell he wouldn't.

He turned and walked towards the door with purposeful strides. 'Keep him alive Doc, until I get back.'

'I'll do what I can.'

'Where are you goin', Chad?' Ira enquired.

'I'm goin' to kill a couple of snakes.'

'Wait for me, son,' the rancher called out.

'Stay here, Pa,' Hunter ordered. 'Help the doc out.'

Before Ira could protest further, his son was gone.

16

Hunter hurried along the boardwalk towards the Elk Horn saloon. A hot fire burned within him as the rage he felt threatened to consume everything. They would not get away with it, he assured himself. Too many good people had died because of the Committee and they deserved justice for their families, for the town. It too had been living under the heel of the four men. Too scared to speak out, the citizens just acceded to the Committee's demands. Now it would all stop. Tonight would be the end of it, or he would die trying. There was no way Hunter would let any more people be hurt by these men.

He stopped outside the Elk Horn's batwing doors and peered over the top of them. Being late in the evening, there were only a handful of customers left. He could not see either Yates or

Johnson. They would be in the back room, he guessed. However, Eustis Lowery sat in the far corner with a two-thirds empty bottle of rye on the table in front of him. Hunter studied him for a moment and concluded that the morose-looking rancher was drunk.

Hunter turned his attention to Harvey the barkeep, who stood behind the bar polishing shot glasses with a white rag he usually kept in the front pocket of his apron. Taking a deep breath, the Bent Fork sheriff pushed through the doors and into the Elk Horn saloon.

Harvey noticed Hunter as soon as he came in and called out, 'Howdy Chad, feel like a drink? It's on the house.'

The room went silent as they all turned their attention to the Bent Fork sheriff.

'Where is he, Harvey?' Hunter asked the barkeep.

Harvey could see by the look on Hunter's face that he would not be swayed. Besides, he didn't hold with what the

Committee were doing anyway.

Harvey sighed. 'They're out in the back room.'

Hunter noticed the barkeep had said 'they'. Which meant both Yates and Johnson. He nodded his thanks to the barkeep and turned to face the table where Lowery sat. 'Don't you go anywhere. I'll be back for you.'

The drunk rancher stared at Hunter through whiskey-soaked eyes, picked up the bottle, gave him a look of disdain and took another swig.

The door to the back room opened. Out walked Hiram Yates and Slade Johnson and they both laughed at some private joke. They were taken aback at the man who stood in the Elk Horn bar room. By all rights, he should have been dead and the fact that he wasn't meant one thing. The others had failed to do their job and were most likely the ones who were dead instead.

Johnson was the first to recover and his hands dived for the brace of Colts he packed. His hands gripped the ivory-handled gun butts and he commenced his smooth draw but no amount of speed would help the gunfighter this night. And as he brought up his six-guns, the expression on his face told those watching that the flashy hired killer knew that he was a dead man.

The edge was with Hunter because the Bent Fork sheriff hadn't come to the saloon to have a showdown with Johnson, but had come here to kill him. When Hunter saw the pair coming out of the back room, he did not give the gunfighter a chance, just drew his gun and fired.

Hunter's Peacemaker barked loudly in the enclosed area of the bar. Four times he fired and each time a small explosion of red erupted from Johnson's body. The shots were so close together that it sounded like a continuous roll of thunder which climaxed with the gunfighter piled in a bloody heap upon the floor at Yates' feet.

'Now it's your turn, you fat son of a

bitch,' Hunter snarled as he shifted aim to cover the shocked Committee leader.

'No, wait,' Yates cried desperately and shrank back from Hunter. 'Please don't shoot.'

'Why the hell should you get a chance, Hiram?' Hunter hissed. 'You ain't never given anybody else none. What chance did you give my brother? What chance did you give Adam Proud? And what about the judge tonight, when you had your gun shoot him down cold? Nope, you deserve what's comin' to you.'

The triple click of the gun hammer going back sounded deafeningly loud in the hushed saloon. Yates stood frozen to the spot, his whole body trembled, terrified of his impending demise.

As Hunter took up the slack on the Peacemaker's trigger, a sharp crack filled the saloon and the Bent Fork sheriff felt as though a mule had kicked him in the back. He fell forward and lost his gun when he crashed onto the timber floor. His body was numb from the impact of the .41 calibre slug that had come from the Colt derringer. The room reeled and far off he could hear a screeching sound. A woman; it had to be a woman, he thought.

Hunter could feel blood running freely from the burning hole in his back. He tried to move but his extremities failed to answer the call. He knew that he had to get his gun. If he didn't he was a dead man. Yates would not hesitate to shoot him.

Finally his right arm moved and he stretched it out towards the fallen Peacemaker. His hand moved tortuously slow, all the time the screech continued. What was it she was saying? Hit the bum . . . No, get the gun. She was screaming for Yates to get the gun.

Hunter renewed his efforts and crept painstakingly closer to the Peacemaker. Just a little further . . . a little further and . . .

A hand with sausage-like fingers scooped the six-gun up before Hunter could close his right hand over the gun butt. He knew of only one man with a hand like that. Hiram Yates.

A mirthless laugh was followed by the relieved voice of the large man. 'Well done my dear. I admire your work, shooting the scoundrel in the back like that when he was about to murder me in cold blood.'

'I couldn't let him kill you, Hiram,' the woman said. 'What else would I do for money?'

'Yes, you're quite right,' Yates agreed. 'Can't let the goose that laid your golden egg die now, can we?'

The voice, thought Hunter, he knew the voice. With sheer willpower he rolled over onto his back. Eyes closed tightly and a low moan escaped his lips as pain shot through his body. He waited for it to subside then opened his eyes. He blinked away the tears that the sharp pain had caused and when the blurriness left, a clear vision of the woman came into view.

She still held the derringer in her small fist. She wore a sky-blue dress and she had long wavy, flowing black hair.

'Son of a bitch,' Hunter cursed out loud. 'You shot me.'

'Damn right I shot you,' Pam Yates spat at him. 'You were about to ruin everything.'

Hunter was confused. 'But why? You don't even love him.'

'You're right,' she allowed, 'and Hiram knows that. But I can still act the good wife and reap the financial rewards that come with it. We stand to be so rich that we could burn paper notes to keep warm of a night and still have enough left over for the rest of our lives. And no one has the right to stand in the way of it. Not even you.'

A wave of pain washed over Hunter and he gritted his teeth until it passed. He focused on Pam and spoke bitterly through gritted teeth. 'I guess I was right in the beginning too, about Buster. You sold us the whole story just so the others could murder my brother.'

'She did what I asked her to do,' Yates cut in.

Hunter's eyes grew cold and hate-filled. 'Then I hope you'll be happy with one another, but remember this, there'll be someone else come along and you will both get what's comin' to you.'

'Enough of this, Hiram,' Pam snapped, 'shoot him and be done with it. Show them all what happens when they interfere.'

Yates lined the Peacemaker up on the centre of Hunter's face, whose gaze hardened as he looked into the gaping hole that was the six-gun's cold steel muzzle. He gritted his teeth but refused to shut his eyes. There was no way he would give the bastard the satisfaction. Hunter saw the whitening of the knuckle as the trigger finger took up the slack.

With all eyes focused on what was about to happen to the Bent Fork sheriff, nobody saw the barrel of the Henry rifle slide up over the batwings and take aim across the room.

The room rocked with the explosion of the rifle being fired. There was a hollow 'thunk' when the bullet hit Hiram Yates in the chest. The big man staggered but didn't fall, his face was a mask of shock and disbelief. The crowd of onlookers heard the next round being jacked into the breech of the rifle and turned to see who the shooter was. Batwing doors swung open; Ira Hunter stepped into the bar room and raised the Henry to shoot again.

'No!' Pam Yates' scream rang out.

Ira took no notice. All he could see was the man who'd murdered one of his sons and was about to do the same to the other. The rifle whiplashed as he fired again. The .44 calibre slug flattened out as it smashed into one of Hiram Yates' ribs, which shattered and deflected the small hunk of lead up into his heart. The big man dropped the Peacemaker and fell heavily to the floor.

'No!' Pam screamed again. 'What have you done?'

She ran to the dead man's side and hunkered down over his prostrate form. Her shoulders trembled as she began to cry. Not for the man, but for what the man had offered her. And now it was all gone.

Ira crossed the floor and crouched beside his son. 'Are you OK?'

Hunter winced and said, 'I think I'll live.'

'Let's get you up and over to the doc's.'

It took a little effort but Hunter managed to gain his feet with the help of Ira and Harvey the barkeep. He looked over at the sad form of the woman he loved, still hunched over and crying silently. He almost felt sorry for her but the thought of what she'd become quickly pushed that aside. Then he thought of the one remaining Committee man, Eustis Lowery. He looked about but the man was gone.

'Come on, son, let's go,' said Ira softly. 'It's over.'

17

Eustis Lowery was found the following day. He'd found a rope at the Bent Fork livery stable and hung himself from one of the rafters. It was the last death of the Stone Creek Valley war. He was buried two days later along with Hiram Yates, Slade Johnson, Jim Hall, Charlie Kemp and Jethro Sharp. All were placed in unmarked graves in the hope all trace of what happened would be erased with time.

Pam Yates was locked up in the Bent Fork jail awaiting trial. She was under the watchful eye of a United States Marshal who had finally arrived and taken over as the town law until Hunter healed.

Hunter's pa was back out at the ranch and had hired some new hands to help while his mother was still in town fussing over her remaining son. He guessed that it helped take her mind off the loss of Buster.

The miracle of it all was Judge Eldred Banks. He'd been called a tough old buzzard once by a cowboy he'd sent to prison for rustling a few head of stock. Well, the cowboy had been right and that 'tough old buzzard' had pulled through under the watchful eye of Doc Hayes, who, every time he looked at him, would shake his head and mutter, 'You should be dead.'

Hunter had the derringer slug taken out of his back and was resting up in bed at the Bent Fork boarding house when there was a soft knock at the door of his room.

'Come on in, it ain't locked,' he called out.

The door swung open with a squeak and standing in the opening was Emma Proud. Hunter was taken a little aback because she was the last person he thought that he would see.

She entered the room but left the door open as she crossed to his bedside.

'I wanted to say thank you for what you've done, especially for Ma and me,' Emma said in her soft tone. 'Now that we have the ranch back we can move all our things back out there and set to running it again.'

'You might want to make a little room for some more cattle,' Hunter told her.

Emma frowned. 'Why?'

'Well, I was talkin' to the marshal that's lookin' after things while I'm laid up,' he explained, 'and seein' as there is a whole herd of cattle that's been bought and paid for comin' into the valley, we agreed that they should be split up amongst the ranchers.'

It was Emma's turn to be taken aback. 'Why would that happen?'

Hunter shrugged. 'Call it compensation for everythin' the valley has been through. I know it won't bring your pa back but . . . '

He left the sentence unfinished.

Emma Proud nodded. 'Well then, thank you. Now I'd best be going, Ma is waiting on me.'

'When I'm back on my feet I'll come out and check on you to see that it's all goin' OK,' Hunter stated. 'You and your ma I mean.'

A tinge of red touched Emma's cheeks as she smiled and said, 'I think I'd like that.'

'Then it's settled.'

As she turned away, Hunter watched her go. He noticed how she moved gracefully across the floor. Just before the door closed behind her, she gave Hunter a warm smile.

'Yes sir,' he thought, 'the Circle P might need a lot of help to get back up and runnin'.'

We do hope that you have enjoyed reading this large print book.

Did you know that all of our titles are available for purchase?

We publish a wide range of high quality large print books including:
Romances, Mysteries, Classics
General Fiction
Non Fiction and Westerns

Special interest titles available in large print are:
The Little Oxford Dictionary
Music Book, Song Book
Hymn Book, Service Book

Also available from us courtesy of Oxford University Press:
Young Readers' Dictionary
(large print edition)
Young Readers' Thesaurus
(large print edition)

For further information or a free brochure, please contact us at:
Ulverscroft Large Print Books Ltd.,
The Green, Bradgate Road, Anstey,
Leicester, LE7 7FU, England.
Tel: (00 44) **0116 236 4325**
Fax: (00 44) **0116 234 0205**

Other titles in the
Linford Western Library:

QUARTER TO MIDNIGHT

Ned Oaks

Brutally attacked one night in the woods, Steve Karner hadn't been seen in years, and everyone in the Oregon town of Stayton thought him dead. Then the men who tried to kill him start dying, one by one; and it soon becomes apparent that Karner is not only alive, but riding a vengeance trail. But there are many dangers to be faced along the way, including a cunning young millionaire who will use all his family's power to protect his secrets, and a cold-blooded hired killer out for Karner's blood . . .

DEAD MAN'S EYES

Derek Rutherford

Ex-train robber Jim Jackson is fresh out of the tough Texas Convict Leasing System, where brutal guards beat all the courage out of him. Now good for nothing except drinking, Jackson is known as 'Junk' by the townsfolk of Parker's Crossing. But Jackson has one thing going for him — he's the fastest gun the Texas Rangers have ever seen. When a series of violent murders terrify the people of Parker's Crossing, it is to Junk Jackson they turn. But can Jackson find the courage to take on the killers?

OUTLAW EXPRESS

Gillian F. Taylor

Sheriff Alec Lawson has infiltrated a band of outlaws in order to capture them — but when they kidnap Lacey Fry from the Leadville express, he breaks his cover in an attempt to bring the young woman to safety. Learning of the betrayal, gang leader Bill Alcott vows to find Lawson and kill him. Lawson doesn't know the territory and he doesn't know Lacey. But the chase is on, through snow and bloodshed, until one of the men can run no further — and hunter and hunted finally come face to face . . .

TAGGART'S CROSSING

Paul Bedford

John Taggart and Jacob Stuckey are Civil War veterans who operate a ferry on the mighty Arkansas River — but trouble still finds them in the tranquil setting. After robbing a bank in Wichita, Russ Decker and his gang's escape route takes them by way of the ferry crossing. Once there, Decker decides to stop pursuit by putting John and Jacob out of business permanently. But fate decrees that a keelboat full of stolen silver ore will arrive at Taggart's Crossing just at the right moment to create maximum havoc . . .

BLAZE OF FURY

Alexander Frew

Tired of being a gun-toting hero to some and a villain to others, ex-bounty hunter Jubal Thorne is looking forward to a peaceful life on his late brother's farm. But when a man has such a past, it isn't long before fate comes knocking on his door. It all starts with a stray bullet that just misses his head, and ends in a blaze of fury. In defence of what is his own, Thorne shows that the bounty hunter might leave his profession, but his profession will never leave him . . .